DRAKE HALL

The Secrets of Ormdale
Book Two

Christina Baehr

Copyright © 2024 by Christina Baehr

Cover illustration and design by Shiloh Longbottom

All rights reserved.

No portion of this book may be reproduced in any form without written permission from the publisher or author.

*For Peirce, my duet partner,
who read my first novel as soon as I gave it to him.*

The multitude of creatures which the earth nourishes
God made for man, with a view to enrich him;—
Some are violent, some are mute, he enjoys them,
Some are wild, some are tame;
the Lord makes them
—Taliesin, from *The Mabinogion*

Chapter One

I was a little late, but still I paused to take a breath outside the door. Crossing the threshold of this room felt like passing into another world—or another time.

It was not wholly an illusion. The hands of the large clock which stood next to me in the passage were quite still; the pendulum motionless. I suspected they had slept like that for years.

A voice came from inside the room. "Edith?"

My hand fluttered up in a habitual but futile attempt to tidy my ridiculous hair. I reminded myself that it never did any good, and opened the door.

The woman who sat in the bed surprised me, no matter how many times I visited her. Her skin was milky pale and her hair was all heavy waves of auburn, with no traces yet of grey.

I always had the impression that she was a queen receiving courtiers; her carved and curtained bed a throne. As was her custom, she wore a loose silk gown just such as the ones that

Pre-Raphaelite enchantresses did; today it was the shade of an overcast sky.

Helena Drake also wore a smile of gentle amusement. "You are late."

"I saw the most extraordinary thing," I said, sitting in my accustomed chair. "A kind of river dragon, I think. Laying eggs in the bank of the river, near the Falls. Look, I've marked the place."

I held out to her my little notebook. This notebook had been left with me by my brother George, with strict instructions as to the kind of observations I must make about all the dragon species that lived in the Dale. I couldn't be expected to keep it as well as he would, of course, but until he returned to spend the summer holidays with us, the notebook would have to put up with me.

George had drawn up a rudimentary map of the Dale for me to mark sightings. This was the page I showed Helena now. She examined it carefully through a lorgnette which she wore on a chain around her neck.

"Ah, yes, I've seen this one many times. But you should have the place marked as 'Foss' not Falls. That is the old Norse word that is used in these parts. And that one has a name, you know."

"Oh?"

"Yes. It is known as Bess's Foss."

"Is it for any special Bess?"

"A very special Bess indeed," she said, with a look of meaning.

"You don't mean…" I trailed off. Helena's son had told me that Queen Elizabeth herself had bestowed this land on his ancestor in recognition of services rendered, though he had been vague about what those services were.

"Yes, I do," Helena answered simply.

"Did she come here?"

Helena nodded. "There is a bedroom here, and even a bed, in which she is supposed to have slept."

"Good heavens!"

At this point there was a soft knock at the door and the Drakes' butler came in with a small animal, which he placed in Helena's arms.

"Thank you, Forrester. I hope Mr. Darcy was quiet and good for his bath."

Forrester bowed and left—noiseless as a shadow. Helena looked after him for moment with softened eyes. Like Gwendolyn, Helena had lost many people close to her. No wonder she was attached to this faithful retainer.

"Mr Darcy bit him once, and poor Forrester wouldn't let anyone tell me about it for a whole day. I was furious when I found out. But it wasn't too late, thank God."

Helena stroked the creature tenderly. It was the general shape and size of a Pekinese dog. But it had colourful scales instead of fur, small useless wings halfway down its body, and (or so it seemed to me) an expression of simmering fury. I had schooled myself not to stare at it, lest I annoy it further, but today I thought it looked if possible even more sour-tempered—no doubt as a result of its involuntary ablutions.

"Ma'am, I've been meaning to ask. What was it exactly that the original Drake did to receive these lands? Why so close to the Abbey of my family?"

"I shall answer your question, Edith. On one condition." She carefully adjusted her lapdragon's collar.

"Yes?"

"That you will answer mine. What are your intentions?" There was a humorous quirk to her lips as she said this.

"My...intentions, ma'am?" I could not imagine what she might be talking about.

Her eyes locked with mine. They were a striking grey, brought out by the shade of her gown.

"Your intentions. Towards my son."

I blushed and burst into a nervous laugh. "Really, ma'am! What have I done to deserve such an interrogation?"

"You must know that you are the first young woman whom Simon hasn't looked upon as a sister."

Despite her bantering tone, I could see she was in earnest.

I sobered. "I suppose I am."

"Well? What do you intend to do?" She tilted her head to one side and waited for my response.

"I can't help thinking I have rather an unfair advantage," I said, stalling, and trying to keep my tone light. "Perhaps Simon should be given the chance to compare me with other women who are also not his sisters, lest he make a hasty choice."

"Unfair advantage? Pshaw! We women must take all the advantages we can. We get so few of them. I for one will never fault you for pressing your advantage."

She then began to speak of other things but my heart was beating quickly and I did not follow them. Helena had as good as told me that Simon was infatuated with me, and that I should press in for the kill, so to speak. This was a most extraordinary conversation to have with a young man's mother. It left me feeling whirled about.

But then, I'd never had an ordinary conversation with Helena Drake. From the first time I had come to see her, this had been so. She was quite unlike anyone I had ever encountered. Perhaps she *was* an enchantress, and I her acolyte. I could not believe that *I* was magical, despite my newfound ability to heal dragon bites, but I could easily believe it of her. There was something about her, and about this house, that belonged more to the fairy books my stepmother had read to me than the England I knew.

A thought sparked in my mind. "Ma'am, you said you would answer my question."

Now she eyed me with a touch of respect. "Well done, Edith. I thought you'd let it slip by."

I felt a glow of pleasure at her praise; she was not a woman to be easily impressed. She went on. "Bartholomew Drake was granted these lands as a gift because whilst on a voyage with his uncle, Sir Francis Drake, he was responsible for the acquisition of a Spanish galleon containing, among other treasures, a rare young dragon of a species found only in the New World."

I sucked in a breath. "Of course! They sent him here because the Worm Wardens were already at the Abbey. And what happened to the dragon? Do you know?"

"I believe it retreated to the caves and it was that which gave Bartholomew Drake the idea of concealing his treasure there. The old legend of dragons guarding gold, you know."

"Yes! His pirate loot. Good gracious, it's like something out of Stevenson, isn't it?"

"We prefer 'privateer', my dear," she said. It was a gentle reproof, but a real one.

"Oh. Of course."

"So now tell me, what is it that makes Ormdale particularly special?"

"You mean besides the presence of dragons and pi— privateers in the middle of Yorkshire sheepland?" I asked.

She nodded.

"Well," I said, lacing my fingers together thoughtfully. "Ormdale already had a respectable population of native dragons, going back to the Middle Ages. And then you told me one of my ancestors was associated with the East India Company and collected Oriental dragons, presumably including an ancestor of your Mr. Darcy, and now you tell me we had at least one American dragon in the 1500s. So I suppose we're a bit of a dragon menagerie. A zoological gardens, if you will, like the Rothschilds' new museum at Tring, except for mythical beasts."

"Hardly mythical," she murmured in faint protest.

There was a pause, in which I realised that Helena had pointedly stopped telling me about family history. Helena's silences were as important as her speeches.

"There's something else, isn't there? Something I missed," I admitted at last, looking up a little ruefully. "Something important."

Helena smiled at me. "But you haven't missed it. It's somewhere in your mind. You'll find it, later."

I knew better than to press her. Confined to this room for many years by ill health, she dwelled in a different kind of time than most of us.

"But ma'am, I wonder if you would tell me about an ancestor of mine I've heard stories of? A woman who drove about with a monkey?"

"Ah yes, Lady Amelia. She was married to Sir Anthony Worms, the East India Company gentleman. He was knighted during the Regency. I knew their son, Barnaby. He was an old man, of course, by then." Her eyes grew unfocused, as if she was entering into a memory fully. "It was he who built the glasshouse at the Abbey as a home for the exotic dragons his father brought back from the subcontinent. I believe Barnaby spent all of his father's money in a few decades, just in building and heating it. But he loved them, you know."

And then I thought that tears came to her eyes for an instant. She smiled at me suddenly, the moment gone. "Well, now. Shall we read?"

This was part of our routine. Helena would pick up whatever novel she was currently reading, and I would take one from my pocket or choose one from her shelves, and we would read in companionable silence until it was time for me to go back to the Abbey for tea.

It felt odd at first, but I grew to enjoy it. Helena's illness did not spare her much energy for movement or even conversation. Sitting quietly together was a way that she could enjoy companionship without being drained. I felt privileged to provide it.

In conversation I felt a little awed by her, and found myself strangely anxious to please her. But in these quiet hours we seemed to settle wordlessly into a kind of comfortable equality. We were, in these moments, no longer mentor and pupil, but simply fellow readers.

I glanced at the volumes already lying on the small table next to me. The outlandish title of one of them sounded a faint note in my mind. *The Mabinogion*. What was it? Something my father had mentioned? I picked it up and read this on the first page:

In the centre of the chamber King Arthur sat upon a seat of green rushes, over which was spread a covering of flame-coloured satin, and a cushion of red satin was under his elbow.

"I wonder where they got all that satin," I murmured. I then spent a happy hour immersed in these Welsh tales of enchanted glades and mountains, auburn-haired beauties, Arthurian knights with unfathomable Welsh names, and mysterious beasts that assisted them on their adventures.

Then I said goodbye to Helena and showed myself out. I was relieved that I did not run into Simon on this visit. After his mother's surprising instructions to 'reel him in' I did not think I could face him until I'd had a little time to reflect.

Our friendship had begun inauspiciously. I had judged him untrustworthy at first sight. His manner and physical appearance (tall, dark, and well-made) marked him as the Byronic hero of a gothic novel. Not at all the kind of young man I intended to marry—if marry I ever did, which I was not at all sure I would. Gothic men, I thought, did not often make good husbands—at least if literature was to be believed on this point.

Instead, I had found him to be kind, humble, and given to unexpected laughter. To be sure, he was a little stilted and old-fashioned in his manners, but that was only to be expected given his upbringing in remote Ormdale. He had won my liking, but not my heart.

As I crossed the river on my way back to the Abbey, I looked back at Drake Hall, glimpsing its elegant Elizabethan lines through the softly whispering trees. It was a very lovely place indeed. And Drake, I had discovered, was a very good man.

In the last two months I had discovered a new family, a new home, and new duties. I was a born healer of dragon poisons. And I was learning to be a dragon keeper. I was even, for the first time in my life, really learning how to be a friend to someone—and if anyone needed a friend, my cousin Gwendolyn certainly did.

I was still finding my footing in this extraordinary place that had suddenly become mine. Now was not the time to lose my head over a man for the first time. No—a love affair was quite out of the question. The very idea tired me!

Simon would have to master his feelings for me. I told myself they were probably no stronger than those which usually accompanied a boy's first infatuation.

I turned away from the hidden valley and climbed up the path to the Abbey.

"It's Whitsunday Eve, Gwendolyn," I said.

"Oh, yes," my cousin responded absently.

"Mother will be arranging flowers for the altar," I continued, mostly to myself as Gwendolyn was clearly not listening. "I usually change the altar cloth and candles. They're always red for Whitsunday, you know."

This was a day I usually spent in ecclesiastical activities appropriate to the dutiful daughter of a clergyman.

I had never before spent it in wiggling a dead rat on a string in the direction of a hungry wyvern. (A wyvern, by the way, is a two-legged winged dragon, both scaled and feathered, about the size of the large Alpine dogs of St. Bernard.)

I had, of course, questioned my cousin Gwendolyn as to the reason behind this ritual the first time we had performed it, some weeks ago.

"Oh," she had said reflectively, "I suppose it's because the wyvern doesn't like to eat dead things."

This had sounded the most reasonable thing in the world. Which worried me a little. Really, the most odd things were becoming commonplace, while everyday things had begun to feel strange.

"Well," I had replied. "I myself prefer to eat dead things. Though it sounds rather macabre when you put it that way, doesn't it?"

Today, however, on the Eve of Whitsunday, I considered myself quite an old hand at feeding mythical beasts deep in the bowels of my family's gothic ancestral home. Perhaps—though I had only discovered it at the age of twenty-one—this really was something I was born to do.

I had spent the last month learning about some of the mysterious objects in the Muniments Room and helping Gwendolyn with any dragon handling tasks that popped up. Now we were getting to the part of the year when the creatures would come out in earnest. It wouldn't just be one lonely wyvern roused from hibernation too early in the year.

In reality, I wasn't yet clear exactly how many species of dragon existed in this Yorkshire valley, especially given yesterday's conversation with Helena. I expected to find out soon. The prospect both excited and intimidated me.

Gwendolyn was sitting on a stool outside the cell I was in with the wyvern, making some notes in a book by the dim light of a lantern on a hook. She was paying little or no attention to me, which I took as generally a good sign.

"Passive indicative!" I called out to test her, while I continued my grim puppetry.

Gwendolyn didn't hesitate. "*Amor, amaris, amatur...*" She chanted the conjugations quite musically from memory, without a complaint.

"Good. Now Greek."

This elicited a very slight groan. Gwendolyn had done surprisingly well in her Latin studies, to which she credited the childhood French her otherwise useless governesses had insisted upon. Unfortunately, she made up for her aptitude for Latin with an inexorable dislike of Greek.

Still, we persisted. Gwendolyn would need a basic knowledge of both ancient languages to successfully sit the entrance examination at the London Medical School for Women, as she hoped to do before the year was out.

The wyvern was watching the stiff rodent jerk about with what I felt sure was suspicion. I tried to make it lively, but the wyvern's bright eye began to look more intrigued by my own gyrations than its dinner.

Suddenly I heard a man's voice call down from the top of the stair that led into the cellars where the holding cells for wayward dragons were located, and which we presently occupied. I couldn't help jumping a little in surprise.

"Miss Worms? It's Alfred. May I come down?" The voice was slow and solid, and deeply of the Dale.

"Yes, yes, please do," called Gwendolyn.

With a snap of the wyvern's powerful jaw the rodent was gone. My jolt of surprise must have lent verisimilitude to the corpse's animation.

"Ah," I sighed and withdrew from the cell, shutting the cell door behind me, relieved to conclude the daily *danse macabre*.

Alfred Dugdale, our new estate Manager, came down the stairs with a heavy tread. He was about forty-five and as solid and expressionless as the Great Rock which stood in the dale. Part of me longed to see him surprised. But I reflected that if wyverns could not succeed in provoking a visible reaction from him, I did not wish to see what could.

"Shepherd's been to see me. Sheep's all safe in upland paddocks."

Alfred often spoke in this abbreviated way. His words, like his features, seemed chiseled in stone.

"Thank you, Dugdale," said Gwendolyn, making a note in her book.

I looked back and forth between them.

"Does that mean we can free the wyvern?" I asked.

"Well, that's a little dramatic, Edith," said Gwendolyn, shutting her book and standing up. "But yes, the lambs are no longer in the immediate vicinity, which will afford them sufficient protection."

I turned to Alfred. "The dragons don't like to go too far into the fells," I said knowingly. "Because of the cold and wind."

Alfred's face was still as a corpse. I thought that he, at least, need never fear being eaten by a wyvern. The rat had more animation.

"But you knew that, being raised in the Dale," I ended weakly.

Despite his lack of small talk I was deeply grateful for his presence on the estate. Gwendolyn had been struggling to run it alone since the sudden death of her father and brother at the end of winter.

Alfred was some sort of cousin to the small family of servants that lived and worked at the Abbey. Because he'd been born and raised in Ormdale, he was aware that the Dale was home to England's last surviving dragons, and that we, the Worms family, were England's last surviving dragon keepers.

He got on well with the shepherds and tenant farmers on our estate and had some new ideas for making the estate financially profitable, something it seemed my ancestors had not bothered much about. He'd lived outside of the Dale for a time, working as a supervisor at the big lime-works in Swallowdale, and I hoped this would give him a fresh perspective on how to solve the estate's pecuniary problems. Sometimes his ideas were a little too fresh for Gwendolyn, who seemed to have cast herself in the role of gatekeeper and preserver of the family traditions.

Gwendolyn and I had next to lead the wyvern up the stairs, down a passage, into the kitchen and from thence into the kitchen yard. It turned out to be much easier than I expected as the wyvern seemed quite happy to simply follow me.

"Why do you think I had you feed it, Edith?" said Gwendolyn, when I remarked on this.

Once in the yard I carefully removed its collar, admiring the revelation of iridescent scales in sunlight.

The gate to the walled kitchen yard was open and I expected it to bolt. Instead, it settled down in the dusty yard like a chicken sunning itself.

A gigantic scaly chicken, with a murderous looking barb on the end of its tail.

"Gwendolyn. It's not going anywhere," I said in a low tone after a moment or two.

"You fed it too much," she accused. "It doesn't want to find its own food now. It knows a good thing when it sees it." She said this with distaste, as if the creature was morally culpable for its lack of enterprise.

Just at that moment a flock of birds flew over the kitchen yard, not much higher than our heads. I was hardly aware they were there before the wyvern stood up, lifted its head and opened its jaws extremely wide, with a bizarre ingressive honk that reminded me strongly of the time my brother George had croup.

What happened next was even more startling. Half a dozen or so of the birds dropped straight into the creature's mouth, as if they'd been sucked out of the sky. The wyvern then snapped its jaws shut and settled down to bask again at our feet.

I was speechless for a moment.

"I don't think I've been feeding it enough."

"Greedy," sniffed Gwendolyn.

"Is it going to live here now? Just outside the kitchen? Won't it make the servants nervous?"

"Edith, the servants are as used to seeing dragons as I am, and a sight more than you are. Besides, it's breeding season now and it will be looking for it's mate. Oh, no!" she exclaimed, voice was full of dread.

"What?" I asked, swinging round to look about me, expecting some alarming creature had made an appearance.

"It's just...you do know about...*all that*, don't you?" Gwendolyn's voice sounded pinched.

She looked so stricken that I quickly guessed what she was talking about. I burst out laughing.

"Oh, Gwen. You do remember that I'm a clergyman's daughter, don't you?"

Gwendolyn blinked at me.

"It's like this," I said, reassuringly linking my arm through hers and walking the two of us back towards the kitchen. "Ever since I can remember, people have been coming to father to confess things," I explained. "I mean, they don't tell me, of course, but one soon figures out quite a lot, especially when it's young girls not much older than oneself. And Mother's always been wonderfully honest with me about *all that*, as you call it."

Gwendolyn looked at me with respect as we stepped into the big kitchen. "Edith. Whenever I think you can't surprise me anymore, you come out with something like that."

I shrugged. "Let's have a cup of tea. You're nervous about Monday, aren't you?"

My particular pet dragon, Francis, saw me as soon as I came into the room. He left his warm spot by the kitchen range to climb deftly up my dress to his customary place on my shoulder.

"Of course I'm nervous! I'm sure Dr Worthing is going to send me packing."

"Well, he'll have to listen to you first. You've made an appointment."

There was a homely teapot on the kitchen table, steaming appealingly. It was most likely intended for us, but one didn't like to make assumptions with these servants, who were the descendants of vikings. (One didn't like to imagine what they might do if really provoked.)

"Cook, might I steal a cup or two?"

Martha, our Cook, waved a hand at me. She wasn't much for niceties, and was currently at the chopping block, cutting up a carcass with grim enthusiasm. (Perhaps I didn't have to imagine.)

I found two cups and poured out while Gwendolyn sat at the table.

"Have I been very horrible?" said Gwendolyn, clasping her cup and looking up at me with her beautiful eyes. Now that I knew my cousin better, I found Gwendolyn's mixture of imperious authority and childlike vulnerability rather endearing. I was no longer intimidated by her air of aristocracy, knowing it disguised her own deep-seated feelings of inferiority.

"You've been a little terse," I admitted. "Have you given any thought to Alfred's proposal for the limeworks?"

Gwendolyn looked guilty.

"Father would have never entertained the thought for a moment. He was totally against any kind of excavation."

I considered this for moment.

"Gwendolyn, your father ran the estate his way for twenty years. And it didn't turn out very well. Why not try your way?"

"And what is my way, Edith?" She set her tea cup down with an exasperated click.

"I don't know. But while you are sorting that out we might try Alfred's. My father hired him in large part so that you could focus on other things," I reminded her gently.

"Simon says the same thing," she snorted.

"I have the greatest respect for Simon's opinion," I smiled, tickling Francis's throat absently.

"Do you? Is that all?" She looked at me sideways as she sipped her tea.

"Is what all?"

"Respect. For Simon."

I glanced at Martha. The kitchen was very large, and she was on the other side of it, thwacking through flesh and bone.

"Is he here today?" I asked.

"He left after I called him a dunderhead. I told you I was being horrible. Anyway, he doesn't mind. He's had to bear with my moods since he was four. He's a perfect lamb about it.

You...you will be kind to him, won't you? Whatever happens? He deserves a little kindness."

"Well, I won't call him a dunderhead," I retorted. And she laughed.

Gwendolyn didn't laugh often, but it felt like striking gold when she did. I had stayed at the Abbey at first for my cousin's sake, so that she might have an opportunity—for the first time in her life—to try something other than running a large country house and chasing dragons. At moments like this, I felt a glow of conviction that whatever precisely the nature of my role here turned out to be, I had made the right choice in staying, at least for now. I had never had a friend of my own age before, and our friendship was a source of great pleasure to me.

I glanced out the window into the kitchen yard. I was pleased to see it was empty. The wyvern had gone in search of its mate.

Chapter Two

Gwendolyn and I were ready early in the morning for our trip to the town of Embsay, the last outpost of civilisation in these Northern wilds.

I left Francis tethered in the cloister herb garden and asked Pip, our housemaid's young son, to bring him some kitchen scraps. Pip had been scribbling with a bit of charcoal on a dirty scrap of paper when I found him. He went pale and screwed up the paper in his hand, but as he did so I caught a glimpse of an impressive sketch of the Abbey tower on it. I made a note to provide Pip with pencil and paper to thank him for watching Francis for me.

The spring air seemed to be making Francis restless; I kept losing him and finding him again in odd places. Perhaps his fancy, too, was turning to thoughts of love. The thought of Simon darted across my brain but I batted it away like an insect. If Simon wanted a mate he could jolly well go looking for one, just like the wyvern. Providing either of them with a mate was no responsibility of mine.

I got into the carriage with Gwendolyn and unslung my leather document bag from my shoulder. Gwendolyn was wearing a wide-brimmed hat with a black veil attached, which was rolled up out of the way. Both of us were still in mourning attire for the deaths of her father and brother. From what I had heard of them, they didn't deserve it.

"Drive on, Thomas," Gwendolyn called out and we were off.

I had been in the carriage almost weekly since I had arrived, whenever the weather allowed us to attend Divine Service at the dilapidated church in the village of Ormby. I had not seen the town of Embsay again since the day I arrived from the South with my parents and brother to claim (or rather, try not to claim) my father's inheritance as unwilling squire of Wormwood Abbey.

I had been more nervous than I had cared to admit to myself that first day, and today I was nervous again, though for a very different reason.

"Edith, what have you got in that bag? You look like a solicitor."

I blushed. "Well, you see, I—I finished my manuscript." This was a little disingenuous of me—I had not only finished it, but made a copy and sent it off to my publisher in London. Just in time for my deadline.

Gwendolyn's face was blank.

"The thing I'm writing all the time?" I prodded.

"Oh! Good for you, Edith!" She beamed at me.

"And you see I sort of wondered...if you— if you'd like to read it?"

I had still not managed to find the perfect time to reveal to Gwendolyn that it was I, her cousin Edith Worms, who was the real published author (under the nom-de-plume "E.W. Fairweather") of her very favourite series of detective novels. The two of us were so busy with the running of the Abbey, and then of course there were our adventures as England's last dragon keepers, and if that hadn't been enough we'd been up to all hours cramming poor Gwendolyn full of dead languages. Which hadn't left me much energy for fireside revelations.

Also, I was ridiculously nervous about what her reaction might be. I had been raised in the bourgeoisie, while my cousin was Landed Gentry through and through. We sometimes had very different notions about what was and wasn't proper. I wasn't sure that penning yellow-back novels populated with corpses and underworld villains would cut the mustard with her, especially since I was now attached to the venerable Worms family of Wormwood Abbey (see Burke's Landed Gentry).

In fact, I had once suggested that my younger cousin Violet might like to read one of the Inspector Green novels (without revealing my connection to them) and this innocent suggestion was greeted with shock. "Oh! Oughtn't she to read *improving* things at her age?" had been Gwendolyn's crushing reply. (I didn't say that having improving books thrust on me as a child by well-meaning parishioners had been precisely what drove me to a life of literary crime.)

But regardless of all that, I was determined that today was the day when I would finally reveal myself. Gwendolyn looked strangely hesitant at my offer of the manuscript. Did she sense my own nervousness?

"It's not—it's not anything to do with Greek, is it?" she said in a low voice, and it was a plea from the very depths of her soul.

"Oh, no. I promise it's not. It's not learned at all. It's quite, quite stupid." It is possible I overstated my case here in my desire to reassure her.

"Oh, good," she sighed. "But Edith, have I never told you? I get terribly sick in carriages."

"Oh," I said, a bit crestfallen.

"I've an idea!" she said brightly. "How about you read it to me on the way? That would be lovely!"

"No. It wouldn't be lovely at all." She looked startled by my tone of deep aversion. I took a breath.

"I'm sorry. Only I can't think of anything worse than having to read one's own novel aloud," I said, hugging the document case close, as if she would make me do it by force.

"Death by *oubliette*?" she suggested with an arched brow.

"Doesn't come close."

"Ah. I didn't know."

We were silent for a moment.

"I am sorry, Edith. Of course I'll read it at home, with pleasure. And how clever of you to write a novel. I can't think how it's done. Do you just conjure it all up, in your head? And then write it down?"

I was speechless. I wasn't sure I could describe how I did it any better than I could comfortably read it aloud to her. All the same, I could see Gwendolyn was making an effort and I really ought to meet her halfway. I hadn't had much practise at friendship with other girls my age, but I was fairly sure that this was the sort of thing that one had to do to keep things running.

I looked out the window at the green countryside and tried to organise my thoughts.

"It's a bit like running the Abbey. There are lots of things in your head at once, lots of things that need doing right away, but some are less urgent, and some you think you can leave for a while until suddenly you realise you oughtn't to have left them at all. And then you've got more work to do because you didn't attend to things at the right time. And some you worry about for no reason and turn out to be quite easy. And then sometimes you have something really lovely to do, and it makes it all worth it."

I looked at Gwendolyn hopefully. My friend was staring at me. Attentive, kind—but utterly mystified. I swallowed my disappointment.

"Never mind. Why don't you tell me about what you're going to say to Dr Worthing. I can pretend to be him and glare horribly at you to quell your spirits, and you can practise on me."

We knocked on the doctor's door precisely ten minutes before the appointment time Gwendolyn had arranged by letter. We were shown into a sitting room where we were greeted by a ladylike woman of about forty or so, who turned out to be the doctor's wife.

"I'm so happy to meet you both," said Mrs Worthing as the three of us sat down together and she poured out tea for us. "I have family in Ormdale, you see. My uncle is one of your tenant farmers. I spent many summers there."

Startled, I studied Mrs Worthing with new eyes. Was Mrs Worthing an initiate into the mysteries of Ormdale? Meanwhile, Gwendolyn and Mrs Worthing knowledgeably discussed yows, tups, hoggs, shearlings (all sheep, if you can believe it), and weather, weather, *weather* for a few minutes, while I watched them closely. I had never thought it possible to talk about sheep or weather so much before coming to Yorkshire.

"It must be so difficult for you to get away from the estate," she said. "Forgive me, my husband is quite ready for you, only I couldn't miss the chance to make your acquaintance."

Dr Worthing now appeared for introductions. As Gwendolyn had explained to me, Dr Worthing had only recently taken over the practise of his predecessor, who had been the doctor of the Worms family for decades. He was as pleasant and well-mannered as his wife, and wore a fashionable large moustache, with a little grey in it. He was so throughly modern and ordinary that I couldn't believe he knew anything about our family dragon business.

Gwendolyn soon went to his office and I was left alone with Mrs Worthing. I am not shy. The role of clergyman's daughter requires careful handling of people from a broad swathe of society. But I had recently become a repository of centuries-old ancestral secrets and I was still feeling my way. Perhaps Mrs Worthing sensed this. She quickly turned the conversation to something simpler: gossip.

"Miss Worms, now I can ask what I really want to know. Has a date been set for the wedding? Or is it too soon after the tragedy to contemplate?"

Wedding? Good heavens, had talk of Simon and myself spread so far? I froze for a moment, then realised that she must be speaking of the defunct engagement between Gwendolyn and Simon. Gwendolyn's tyrannical father had intended them for each other since infancy, without reference to their subsequent feelings about the matter. I quickly regained my footing.

"Mrs Worthing, I believe that engagement was something my *uncle* desired. My cousin was willing to please her father while he lived, but now that he has passed away there is no longer any reason for it. Mr Drake has kindly released her from the obligation."

"That was very good of him," she remarked. "It will not be easy to find a young woman equipped to run such a remote house as Drake Hall. Ormdale ways are not to everyone's taste, I think." She looked at me with a perceptive expression. "It would not be an easy life for anyone who wasn't born to it, I think. There are...unique challenges."

I got the impression that Mrs Worthing was sizing me up for the job and felt mildly resentful of it. But I had leaned something from her speech—I now felt sure that at least some draconic encounters had featured in Mrs Worthing's childhood summers in Ormdale. And that gave me an idea.

"Mrs Worthing, might I confide in you?" I asked, setting my tea cup down.

Her eyes brightened. "Why, yes, of course, Miss Worms. As a doctor's wife I am the soul of discretion."

I might have doubted that, but for the fact that Mrs Worthing had clearly not spread the Ormdale secrets abroad. At any rate, in this matter I had little to lose from confiding in her and much to gain.

"My cousin Gwendolyn is an exceptional young woman. She is clever and determined. Animated by the highest motives, she has set her mind on pursuing a vocation in the medical profession."

I now saw proof of Mrs Worthing's discretion as she hardly reacted at all to this news; on the contrary, she listened calmly.

"She has not come to your husband for her own health. She is hoping to secure his help to prepare for the entrance examination of the London Medical School for Women."

Her eyes were now a little veiled. Ah well, I had not really dared to hope for an outright declaration of alliance. But she might yet do something for Gwendolyn's cause, I thought, given time.

I continued. "Of course, I do not expect to draw you out on the subject of your husband's opinions regarding the medical profession. That would be quite impertinent. But I felt with your connections in Ormdale, you might like to understand the arrangement my cousin and I have arrived at."

"Arrangement?" Her eyes were keen again.

"I am taking over much of Gwendolyn's role at the Abbey so she can devote herself to study. And we have taken on an estate manager, which was long overdue. Perhaps you know of him? Alfred Dugdale."

"Oh, yes! So he has finally left the limeworks in Swallowdale? His aunt will be glad of that." She was relaxing again as she was now on neutral ground. "Alfred was always telling her he was not at all satisfied with the working conditions for the men. That rather disturbed her, you know. When one's only nephew is working with explosives every day…"

My work was done. I relaxed into listening to her harmless circulation of tidbits.

A quarter of an hour or so later, we heard voices in the passage.

"Ah, that will be your cousin." She got up and led me into the passage where Gwendolyn was taking leave of Dr Worthing. Gwendolyn had let down her veil, so I could not make out her expression. Dr Worthing took her hand.

"Don't hesitate to tell me if there's anything else I can do for you, Miss Worms."

She nodded and murmured some words of thanks and we were outside on the doorstep. The door shut behind us.

"Gwendolyn?" I ventured.

"Don't. Not here," she said shortly. We had arranged with our servant Thomas to walk a short distance to the inn where we were to dine. The carriage would be waiting there also.

I followed Gwendolyn there, my spirits sinking. We went inside and were shown to a small private parlour. When we were alone, Gwendolyn threw back her veil and let out a sob. There were tears on her face.

"Oh, Gwen. Don't despair. Was it very bad?"

"It was awful." She sat down heavily.

"Horrible man!" I exclaimed.

"No, he was kind. That made it worse somehow. I felt like a child. A foolish child."

"But he absolutely refused to help you?"

"Yes. He said that he couldn't in good conscience encourage me at all on my chosen path. He said my upbringing rendered me completely unfit for such a profession."

"Nonsense!"

"Perhaps he's right."

I took her hands in mine firmly.

"Gwendolyn, he doesn't have the least idea of your upbringing. I'd like to see how *his* nerves are after a night of chasing a deadly wyvern through a dark ruin. And trapping it!" Then

I paused. "His wife would understand better. I've an idea our cause isn't quite lost yet. Let's put our hope in God and Mrs Worthing and eat something. Our spirits may be beaten, but our bodies are defiant."

We ate a subdued meal together. Gwendolyn did not respond to any of my tentative attempts to lighten the mood. If anyone could make things better, it was Mother. What would she do if she were here with us?

We had a few errands in Embsay, to which we now attended. I slipped away, claiming an errand of my own, while Gwendolyn was busy clearing some long-standing debts at the grocer's.

My cousin's exalted family had not been very reliable in such matters for some time, and Gwendolyn was relieved to finally be able to pay them, instead of always putting them off, as had been her father's habit. (I have never understood why the upper classes of this country think it no shame to cheat tradesmen. They would never think of refusing to pay their own servants. As far as I can tell, it is just as reasonable for the grocer to wish to be paid for his candied peel and mouse traps as it is for me to wish to be paid for my books, and my deceased uncle to be paid the rent by his tenants.)

I hot-footed it back to Dr Worthing's and asked to see his lady for a moment. This, I thought, was what Mother would do, though I was sure she'd do it ever so much more delicately than I. Mrs Worthing came quickly and asked if I had left something behind.

"Dear Mrs Worthing, I beg you to hear me out. We have only just met, but I feel quite sure you are a woman of both sense and feeling." She looked surprised and gratified at this. "Please, ask your husband to reconsider. I feel sure he must trust your judgement above anyone's. If he would only give my cousin a trial, a chance to prove her mettle." She seemed about to protest. I lowered my voice meaningfully. "As you say, Ormdale has *unique challenges*. My cousin is not just any squire's daughter, Mrs Worthing, and you know it."

Her lips compressed. I was not sure whether it was with disapproval or determination, but she shook my hand with a firmness that was heartening. I left her and found my way back to Gwendolyn. Our business was concluded within the hour, and we went to meet John who was to have the carriage ready. We were getting in it for the return journey when a boy ran up with a package and note addressed to Gwendolyn.

We glanced at each other in surprise. A spark of hope flickered in Gwendolyn's eyes.

"I'll open the package, you open the note," I commanded. She nodded.

I quickly untied the string and removed the neat brown paper to reveal a prodigious volume entitled *Gray's Anatomy*. A little gasp came from Gwendolyn, such as another girl might make over a new hat.

"Edith, hear this:

Dear Miss Worms, I hope you will forgive me for my hasty words of this morning. Please accept this volume with my com-

pliments. When you wish to discuss its contents, please arrange another appointment by letter. I remain

Your faithful servant, Albert Worthing."

We stared at each other.

"Hip-hip hoorah for Doctor Worms!" I shouted and hugged her, the two of us laughing into each other's shoulders.

Chapter Three

In the excitement of this victory, my manuscript was forgotten. On the way home, I wove a different story instead—a story of Gwendolyn's future medical distinctions. The following morning I took the manuscript out of the document case and put it back in my desk in my own octagonal study at Wormwood Abbey, just a little wistfully. I had always enjoyed my parents' hearty congratulations when I finished a novel, along with some small treat for tea (currant buns were a favourite), and I had not realised before how much this small ritual meant to me.

I went and checked on Gwendolyn. She was in her room, head down in anatomy, and hardly noticed me peering in the door. I felt a little at a loss, like a mother hen whose chick has gone walking alone in the barnyard for the first time and without noticing her mother isn't with her.

I threw myself into my duties. After a conference on some household details with Cook, during which I made sure to ask her to send up a luncheon tray for Gwendolyn, I dressed myself for the outdoors and went out. I was well equipped with a mackintosh, stout boots, a walking stick, and my dragon notebook in my pocket. I did not take Francis with me, because I planned to do some naturalistic observations, with which he might interfere. He had lately manifested a delight in swimming, and I did not want him alarming the river dragon whose nesting habits I wished to observe.

I climbed down into the valley which lay at the foot of the Abbey and made my way along the path which follows the river.

The Orme River was the dividing line between the land belonging to my family's estate and that of the Drakes of Drake Hall. This hidden valley was a magical place that charmed all of my senses. The wildflowers were blooming in a fragrant, profligate tangle, birds darted to and fro, and the river sang to me. My eye caught the jewelled flash of a kingfisher. I breathed it all in and felt myself well repaid for the loss of the currant buns.

I made for the waterfall which Helena had called Bess's Foss, moving stealthily lest I disturb the nesting dragon I had observed there three days ago.

I found myself a good observation spot on the bank opposite and crouched down to wait in the rivergrass, leaning a little on my stick.

My purpose was to try and discover if this river dragon was the kind of creature that left its young to fend for itself, or guarded it from a short distance.

I had been there for perhaps half an hour when I heard or sensed a creature of some sort approaching. I was partly screened by vegetation, but I held myself very still.

On the river path there was a blur of brown behind the foliage of the young trees and Simon's fine bay mare emerged, led by Simon Drake himself.

I stifled a sound of annoyance as he led the horse to the river's edge for a drink. They were not close enough to the nest that I feared for the eggs, but it was unlikely the mother dragon would emerge now.

If only they would leave soon and not hang about. Of course, it wasn't Simon's fault; I'd not seen him to tell him of the nest as yet. He would certainly have kept his horse away if I had.

I watched him stroke the horse's neck as it drank. Simon's hair was as dark as his horse's mane. I had not noticed before how well his skin looked in the sun. It was olive, an almost Mediterranean complexion, nothing at all like his mother's milky one.

The way he interacted with the horse was quite beautiful. One smooth, seemingly effortless movement landed him in the saddle, though the horse was a tall one.

I felt a pang of envy. I had never sat on a horse. I felt sure that if I did, I would look nothing at all like Simon.

As he directed the horse back onto the path, Simon led the horse with a quiet grace that filled me with admiration. It was like watching two musicians playing a duet they knew well. No bluster, no wasted movements. Just a calm communion that could only be based on trust.

At that moment he looked up and our eyes met across the river. Embarrassed at being caught staring at him from amongst the reeds, I used my stick to stand up too quickly. I didn't realise that I had lost circulation to my legs. They gave a terrific wobble.

And then I landed in the river.

I was up and sputtering in shock by the time he got to me.

"Miss Worms, are you all right? Forgive me for startling you."

He strode unhesitatingly into the water and took my arm, gently supporting me as I waded out.

"Oh, dear," I said, once I was on the riverbank, realising how very wet I was. I unpinned my dripping hat and shook it. Simon held it while I wrung water out of my skirts. Fortunately my notebook was unharmed, thanks to the mackintosh.

"Please, come and dry yourself at the Hall," he offered.

Once before, when he had found me in this valley—every bit as lost as the one hundredth lamb—I had refused the enticing prospect of a hot fire and soft chair at his house. This time, I gratefully accepted.

"You must think me a complete ninny," I observed as we rejoined his horse and followed the path together. "This is the second time you've had to come to my rescue here."

"Hardly," he said. "You forget that it was you who saved my life."

"I suppose I did." It hadn't been particularly heroic of me. Since I was a Marsi, a healer of dragon poisons, I had only been obliged to spit in a rather undignified manner on the dangerous bite the startled wyvern had given him.

"Would you be more comfortable riding? I could help you into the saddle." He gestured to the horse.

"I've never sat on a horse in my life," I said, a little ruefully, as I looked up at the enormous animal, a little intimidated by its size and mercurial grace. How curious that I felt more at ease with dragons.

"You astonish me," he said.

"I do?"

"Well...you seem to be able to do everything else."

I laughed. "Everything else but stand on my own feet on a riverbank, you mean!"

He smiled, and turning to the horse made a distinctive low whistle and patted its flank. The horse responded immediately, trotting off down the path ahead of us alone. It had soon disappeared.

"What was that?" I stopped in surprise.

"I told her to go home," he said simply.

"Just like that?" I asked in wonder.

He smiled.

"Was it you who trained Pilot, as well?" I asked suddenly.

"Yes."

"Then you have also saved my life, and we are even," I said, holding out my hand to shake his. "I would never have left those caves alive had it not been for Pilot."

He grasped my hand and released it. His grip was a pleasant one, neither too timid nor too forceful. We continued walking.

"And now you simply must call me Edith," I declared.

"Must I?"

"It's too silly to call me Miss Worms when we are cousins—of some sort—and you have drawn me out of the reeds like baby Moses."

"I would be honoured. Edith."

I was slightly taken aback by the way he said my name. Very carefully, as if he was speaking the name of a saint at her shrine. Good heavens, was it really as bad as that?

I covered my embarrassment by chit-chat the rest of the way to the Hall. I hoped my nonsensical chatter might expedite my removal from any saintly pedestal. It would surely be hard to maintain reverence for a chattering saint dripping with river weeds.

When we arrived at the Hall, Forrester was waiting for us, a shadow at the open door. He must have seen the mare return alone and worried about his young master.

"It's all right, Forrester. Miss Worms slipped into the river, but there's no harm done."

"I'll send someone to the Abbey for some dry things, sir."

We entered the coolness of the building and I shivered. Simon quickly divested himself of his coat and put it round me.

Forester spoke to me directly. "There is a fire in my lady's sitting room, Miss." I saw he meant me to follow him there.

Simon made a hesitant movement. I looked at him questioningly. There was a deep regret in his dark eyes.

"My mother—is not well today."

Like many invalids, Helena Drake had better and worse days. Apparently today was one of the worse ones.

"I will be as quiet as a mouse," I assured him. I vaguely knew that there was a little sitting room which adjoined her bedroom, but I had never seen her use it.

Forester took me upstairs and left me alone in the room, saying he would send a maid to help me.

I went straight to the fire-side. As I began to peel off my soaking layers, I cast a glance around the room.

I paused, surprised by what I saw.

Everything was laid out as if a person of many interests and pursuits had gone out, to return at any moment. There was a small easel with a watercolour paint box and charcoal pencils at the ready. Her work box sat within easy access of what must have been her favourite chair. There was even an embroidery frame, with a beautiful piece of tapestry work, half done.

Yet Helena had told me she had scarcely left her bed in a decade.

I blinked tears. This room represented a part of Helena's life which was gone. Yet it was kept ready for her, day after day, year after year, even down to the meticulous dusting of the half-finished fancy-work. Was it on Helena's orders, I wondered? Was there a devoted family servant who did it all? The personality behind this room must have a steadfast fidelity. Forrester, perhaps? His attendance on Helena had a courtly air about it.

The maid arrived to help me remove my wet clothes. Fortunately, my underthings were only slightly damp and that was solved by sitting quite close to the fire.

There was a tinkle of a bell from the next room. The maid left to answer it and came back a few minutes later with her arms full of some soft and rich fabric.

"Please, Miss, Madam has said you should put this on while you wait for your dry things to come from the Abbey."

She laid the dress over the settee. I caught my breath.

It was one of Helena's gowns, but not one I had ever seen her wear. Having been in mourning for several months, I was starved for colour, and this one made my heart quicken.

The dress was of moss-coloured velvet and had a square neckline embroidered with gold leaves the colour of ripe wheat. The waist was high and softly gathered. It had a slight train which made it feel something that might be seen in a romantic vision of King Arthur's court. I might be Queen Guinevere in this gown. My fingers tingled with desire as I touched it.

I could see the maid was worried that I would refuse, but her fears were misplaced.

"Yes, thank you, I shall," I answered her with a smile.

"And she sent this as well." She held out a comb. I looked at it curiously. It was rather large, with wide-set teeth. It was not the kind of small decorative comb which was fashionable to wear in one's coiffure at that time, and I wasn't quite sure what to do with it. "I'll help you with it, Miss. It's what Madam uses on her own hair."

I felt a foolish throb of hope, which I attempted to quell. My hair was a riddle which I had long ago given up trying to solve. I brushed it faithfully every night, and every morning I awoke to a head that looked like a bird's-nest. I admired Helena's rippling auburn tresses devoutly. I could not believe that mine would suddenly become magically biddable under the influence of a new comb.

But why not? I had felt the first time I visited this valley that it was under an enchantment. Perhaps I might let myself fall beneath its spell—if only for a day.

The maid combed and arranged my hair low and loose on my neck in the manner of a pre-Raphaelite model of my parents' generation. I had a soft spot in my heart for the pre-Raphaelite painters, as they seemed to like women with hair my colour, and depicted them not as saucy shepherdesses or beggars but as queens and even as the mother of Our Lord.

I had no mirror. I could only gaze at the fire while she did my hair, and trust. But I told myself it was all part of the enchantment. Perhaps I was in the house of the prince who had been turned into a Beast, where the servants were magical ones. Perhaps I was being transformed from a small and rather ordinary red-headed rector's daughter into the heroine of a fairy tale.

The maid spoke to me softly. Indeed, everyone in this house was remarkably soft-spoken, which added to the quality of enchantment that hung about it. "I'm done, Miss."

There was a knock on the door and Forrester's voice came to us. "Sir is asking if you would be pleased to come down to dine with him, Miss?"

Was it midday already? Then I realised I was hungry, and that I *did* want to leave the room and be seen in this gown, which fit me marvellously and was more comfortable than my ordinary clothes.

Why was there some strange familiarity to all of this? But of course. The Beauty was required to dine with her host. That was how the story went.

I smiled to myself and followed Forrester down to the dining room.

Chapter Four

I was shown into the dining room at Drake Hall. This was a room I had not yet visited.

The dark wood panelling was carved with flowers and fruit, so rounded and ripe that it was tempting to try and pluck them. The proportions of the room were small but perfect. There was a soft-coloured tapestry on one wall, simply and elegantly worked with a pattern of birds in a tree.

The room was a little dark, which only made the brightness of the mullioned window more dazzling, while the silver on the dining table gleamed.

I didn't see Simon at first. But then he stood, scraping his chair back. His expression recalled the way he had looked at me the first time we met.

At the time, I had been deeply offended to have an unknown young man staring at me so intensely. Now that I knew his odd upbringing and how little society Simon had encountered, I was more patient. And I presumed that my appearance in his mother's dress had startled him.

"This is a delightful room," I remarked, as Forrester seated me opposite Simon and left us. "Your mother made this tapestry, didn't she? It's so much nicer than the ones we have at the Abbey."

"Yes," he answered.

"She must have been very industrious, before her illness."

"Everything seemed to interest her," he smiled. "Books, embroidery, music, paints, plants...and dragons, of course."

"Of course?"

"She is a Marsi, like you. As I understand it, a Marsi can't help being drawn to them. Is that right?"

"I don't know that I feel drawn to them exactly...I just...don't feel repelled at all. They are such strange creatures, and yet they are not strange to me."

He was watching me closely again, as if everything about me interested him deeply. I quickly turned the conversation away from myself.

"And you?"

"Me?"

"Yes, Simon. You. You like animals."

His brow furrowed. "Is that unusual?"

I laughed. "My brother likes animals, certainly. He is a born naturalist. For him they are like living answers to his questions about the world. But I don't think that's what they are to you. Take your lovely mare, for instance."

"Portia."

"Portia. What is she to you? A curiosity to be investigated, like she would be to my brother? A question that leads to other questions?"

He seemed to think for a moment.

"A friend," he said simply.

"You see, I am right. That's what gives you the ability to train them. It's a gift. Did you get it from your father?"

The smile on his face vanished. I instantly regretted the question.

"No. My father and I had very different ideas about how to train animals."

Oh, dear. Was it something in the water that made all the fathers of Ormdale dreadful? I myself had a very loving father who had thankfully left early enough to escape drinking of the waters of the Orme.

"Do not mistake me," he spoke carefully. "My father was a good man. But we did not understand each other very well. And that is something I regret."

Our conversation was interrupted by the dinner being brought in.

We ate quietly for a few minutes. The silence in the house was absolute. We might have been in a dim cavern under the sea.

"It took me weeks to put my finger on why time feels different in this house. It's the clocks. They're all stopped, aren't they?"

He paused, fork in hand. "I suppose it's very odd," he admitted.

"Dickensian, I should say."

He gave a low laugh. "They weren't stopped for any tragically abandoned wedding, if that's what you mean."

I smiled, pleased. Simon seemed to unerringly catch my allusions to novels. He never made slighting comments about them, either, as most of the more learned men I had known were given to do.

"My mother's illness makes her very sensitive to noise. She suffered from sleeplessness for years. The stopping of the clocks brought her some relief."

"I see. Of course."

"The servants have their own working clocks, of course, below stairs. As for myself, I have become used to telling the time from the position of the sun."

There was a sharp, startling noise. We both looked up. It came from the window.

A creature that looked like a rather large hummingbird was bashing against the dining room window from the outside.

"Gracious!" I exclaimed.

Simon stood up and walked to the window.

"It's mistaken it's reflection for a rival," he observed.

"Simon!" I wiped my hands on my napkin with growing excitement. "Is that—"

"Yes. It's a dragon. I believe this belongs to the smallest of the species in the Dale."

I got up and followed him to the window.

Its wings were a blur of unimaginable speed. It had a long, tubular snout. It was brilliantly and iridescently coloured, like a kingfisher or a dragonfly, in orange and sapphire. If I had seen it in my peripheral vision, I would have mistaken it for a bird. Observing it closely, it reminded me of something between a hummingbird and an airborne sea-horse. Its eye seemed to fix on me with an expression of unspeakable rage, but I knew it was only seeing its own reflection, for which it had conceived a fierce enmity.

"How extraordinary!" I whispered. "Won't it exhaust itself?" I felt a rush of concern. "What if it's rival is even now taking advantage of its absence to insinuate itself into the female's affections?"

Simon laughed. He lifted the catch and gently swung the window outwards. The tiny dragon disappeared in a flash of colour.

"They fight each other, you know. It's quite a sight. A sort of aerial duel."

"Don't laugh at them! It's completely serious for them, a matter of life and death!" I remonstrated, but I was half joking myself.

"Yes, it is. But I can't help thinking they would save themselves considerable pain if they let her choose which of them she preferred."

"And when have men been content to do that?" I scoffed. "Half of the myths and stories in the world would never have existed if mankind had followed that doctrine. Think of it—no Troy, no Camelot..."

"Much the better. Far fewer wars."

I sat at the table again. Simon pushed my chair in for me.

"And far fewer epic stories," I countered, out of sheer mischief since I really agreed with him.

Simon sat at the table again, his lips twitching with suppressed laughter. I couldn't resist teasing him, since he took it so well.

"Well, you sound sensible enough, but I'm quite sure when it comes to it you'll fight for the woman you love." I picked up my fork again and made a comic gesture as if it was a sabre. "I look forward to seeing you prove yourself wrong, Simon."

His amused smile remained but his eyes were serious as he answered me.

"I can't imagine accepting a love that's forced or constrained," he said. "And I've never been much of a fighter, I'm afraid. I suppose I'll have to wait for someone who will freely choose me, just as I am."

We'd been joking with each other, but suddenly we were trembling on the brink of becoming entirely too serious—for my comfort, at least. I felt I had taken my teasing a hair too far.

I hummed a few measures of a tune. He looked at me quizzically.

"It's the hymn, you know? 'Just As I Am'?"

He looked blank. I laughed wryly.

"I suppose I have a more encyclopaedic knowledge of them than you do. I am a clergyman's daughter, after all."

"You aren't at all what I imagined a clergyman's daughter to be," he said, his smile reaching his eyes this time.

"And you aren't anything like the gouty Yorkshire squires I imagined. By all means, let us go on surprising each other. It's a pleasant attribute in a friend, don't you think?"

"Very," he agreed warmly.

Afterwards we went up to the Gallery to see the family pictures. Simon had long ago promised to show me a pair of portraits; our mutual ancestors.

When I saw them, I was vaguely disappointed. I could see nothing in them that either of us might have inherited, so far as physical characteristics went. Drake was far too dark and melancholy, and I was too redheaded and determined. These fair, languid people with undecided chins did not seem like our kin.

The picture of the piratical ancestor Helena had told me about, however, delighted me.

"Ah! This must be Bartholomew Drake," I said.

Simon glanced at me quickly. "My mother told you about him?"

"Yes, though not as much as I'd like to know. I wish they'd painted him with his dragon. But I suppose that wouldn't do, would it?" I mused. "How good you all must be at keeping secrets."

Simon made no reply to this.

Bartholomew looked very lordly in his lace ruff and padded pantaloons, posed beside an unusual terrestrial globe that looked as if it had been carved from ebony. "Oh, the globe! His uncle Sir Francis must have taken him along for the ride?"

"On the circumnavigation? Yes."

"*That* would have been something! I suppose it makes up for the missing dragon." There was a shadowy masculine figure in the picture's background, dressed very plainly. "Who is that?"

"One of his spoils, in a way."

Startled, I glanced at Simon.

"Well, not an actual slave," he answered my look. "I believe the figure was painted in after the capture of a Spanish treasure ship. That's what made his fortune."

"Some of which came out of the cave in George's pockets." I was slowly putting it all together; this web of history, secrets, and legends. "Piracy upon piracy!"

"To answer your question, there was a native from the Americas on the Spanish galley. He'd been kidnapped by the Spaniards. Bartholomew brought him back to England with him, and eventually here, to this house, when he built it. I believe the man became his valet."

"But why put your valet in a portrait?"

"I suppose not many Yorkshire squires had a valet that was one of the Aztecs."

"You mean they put this equatorial individual in the picture instead of a treasure chest or something more obvious? To the victor, the valet?"

To my satisfaction, he didn't feign laughter at my rather awkward joke, but simply nodded. We both looked at the picture, sobered.

"Well, I daresay being a valet was better than being a galley-slave," I reflected.

"I very much hope so," was his cryptic response. And we went on to another picture.

When my clean things arrived from the Abbey, I returned the green gown rather sadly. I had felt very different in it, but at the same time oddly more myself while wearing it. I felt a little deflated putting my own things back on: they looked very dull and drab beside its gleaming velvet folds.

I said goodbye to Simon and chose to walk home alone. I had enjoyed my visit with Simon very much, but I felt a little worn from the effort of keeping up a light tone with someone I suspected of having tender feelings for me.

I analysed my conduct towards him while I walked home. Had I been too familiar? I decided that I had not. Simon was a cousin of mine (though a distant one), a close family friend, and the only person in the Dale who was considered a social equal to myself and Gwendolyn.

Besides, if I became suddenly distant, it might only add fuel to the fire of his devotion. Far better to replace the imaginary sainted Edith of his imagination with the real everyday Edith who teased and disagreed with him over dinner. I appreciated his friendship and hoped to keep it, if only he could be weaned off seeing me as a romantic prospect. Quite apart from my own disinclination for a love affair, there was what was best for Simon himself to consider. I might have been joking when I told his mother that he ought to have the opportunity of choosing from an assortment of young ladies, but there was truth in it. Who would want to be loved simply because there was no one else in sight, like the poor nurse in the comic opera? What was it Helena had said about *pressing my advantage*? This was one I had no wish to exploit.

As I came within sight of the Abbey, I impulsively decided to go for a quick walk across the pastures in the direction of the Fells. It looked like rain, but I had my mackintosh on. The light was quite beautiful and I wanted to walk off my dinner before teatime.

I had not gone more than two miles when it began to rain. I pulled up the collar of my mackintosh. Not far from me across the pasture stood an old stone barn. These structures appeared semi-regularly in the landscape, in varying states of disrepair. I made a dash for it as the rain got harder.

Seeking shelter inside, I sat on what appeared to be an old milking can near the entrance and got out my notebook.

George had made columns for recording details about dragon species. I described as well as I could the tiny 'dragon-bird' I had observed after lunch, marking its habits as *diurnal* since I had seen it active during the day.

I began to be aware of an unexpected smell that was present with me in the barn. Smoke. Now that my eyes had adjusted better to the dimness I turned and surveyed the interior. There was a darker discolouration on the earth floor. Before my mind construed what it was, I felt a soft thrum of warning.

Someone had recently made a fire not far from the doorway. Reaching out to touch the place, I found it was not warm, but the smell was strong. I examined the can I had been sitting on and found faint traces of food in it. That a shepherd would keep himself warm and fed was not strange, but I knew from Dugdale that the sheep had been moved to higher ground days ago. These signs were far more recent.

I began to feel slightly chilled, and it was not the weather that made me feel so. I wished my venomous pet dragon was with me.

In most places, the transient signs of a common vagrant or travelling tinker would be of little concern. But Ormdale was a world unto itself. Strangers did not come here, much less onto the grounds of the Abbey itself.

Ever since Gwendolyn and I had discovered that the solicitor Rivers had been hired by an anonymous employer to gather evidence of dragons, we had lived with this unwelcome expectation. We had made no progress in discovering the identity of the mysterious figure behind Rivers's investigations. We suspected that someday, he would send someone else to finish the job; someone who would want to see, and would not want to be seen. This barn would provide the ideal place for such a person to spy out the land.

My reverie was interrupted by a rustling. I jumped up, but calmed when I saw the culprit: a mouse, hiding in the scattering of straw.

While I hoped there was some innocent explanation for what I had found, I was not sorry when the rain lessened a little and I could walk back to the Abbey. I had no wish to encounter a dragon hunter alone and unarmed.

Chapter Five

I found Gwendolyn standing at her bedroom window gazing out of it. The anatomy book was lying on her desk, open, and it looked as if she had already begun scribbling notes, bless her.

"Goodness," I said, flipping through the volume. "Do I really have all of this inside me?"

"No. Some of it's on the outside," she answered.

I approached her. "Is everything all right? Are you crying?"

She turned to me, and her face was certainly damp. But she was standing straight and tall.

"You'll think me a fool. It's only...it's so beautiful. And I never knew. Every bit of it, everything you don't see. Utterly beautiful."

"Oh, Gwendolyn!" I hugged her in triumph. It was as I thought—she *was* made to be a doctor!

"It's even worth learning Greek," she declared recklessly.

"I'm so glad!" I saw the tray of food I'd ordered for her—untouched. "You naughty child, you missed lunch. See what happens when I'm gone."

"I'm ravenous now. Where were you?"

"I fell into the Orme trying to spot the river dragon."

"Fell into the Orme!"

"I know! Fancy letting me out alone. But Simon saved me, dried me, and fed me. So you needn't worry."

"Dried you!" she emphasised.

"Not himself, you goose. I had a lovely time. And before you say anything arch to me about it, I've decided to inoculate him. There's some medical jargon for you!"

"Edith, sometimes I really can't follow you at all," she said, sitting down.

"Inoculate him—towards me."

"And how will you do that?"

"By being my own ordinary, ridiculous self. He's got some idea that I'm a saint, or a heroine, or something. I've decided the best course of action is to expose him to the virus, which in this case is myself."

Gwendolyn eyed me with a somewhat unreadable expression.

"Genius," she remarked. "I'll call you Jenner from now on."

"Jenner?"

Gwendolyn clapped her hands together and almost crowed in triumph.

"Finally, something you don't know! It was Edward Jenner who invented inoculation, of course. For the pox."

"Gwendolyn," I said, drawing myself up to my full height (which was not much). "You are about to fill your head with volumes of things I don't know. I do hope you are not going to be unbearable about it."

"I won't," she said humbly, "It's just my poor education. I often feel like you're leagues ahead of me in everything."

"How nice of you to be my friend anyway." I took her hand and squeezed it. "I'm going to go down to the kitchen and see if tea is almost ready. You dry your eyes and I'll see you in the parlour in a bit."

When I arrived in the kitchen Cook was cutting up potatoes and turnips for pasties. Pip was peeling a pile of potatoes and dropping them into a pail of water. Lily was arranging things on the tea tray. The heavenly spicy-sweet smell of Yorkshire gingerbread, known as *parkin*, filled the kitchen. I was not particularly surprised to see Francis near the range, clearly anticipating the gingerbread.

"Oh, good, I see tea's almost ready. I need to ask you all something."

Three faces looked up. They bore a strong family likeness. Strong, stoic visages all. Pip differed from the rest of his family in having dark hair rather than straw-coloured, but he had the same expression. I imagined it was the same expression the Vikings wore when they invaded Yorkshire and went about pitilessly burning down villages.

I had not made much progress in getting to know them. The separation between classes at Wormwood Abbey was much wider than that I had been used to in my middle-class rectory. I knew only the relationships between them: Martha, our Cook, was married to Thomas, who did all of the heavy work of the household, and whose father John was gardener, and drove the carriage to church once a week (except when the roads were too muddy). Their daughter Lily acted as a maid-of-all-work, and her young son helped with odd jobs. I had never heard tell of a husband for Lily, but I supposed there must have been one once. She was a handsome young woman, in her way. But where would she find a suitor in this remote place? Or, indeed, half an hour in which to walk out with him?

It was a scanty crew for such a big house, and I knew the demands on them were too high. I planned to put on more staff once the estate's finances were in better order.

"I took shelter in one of the old barns in the pastures today. Someone had been cooking over a fire there."

Martha put the pan of parkin on the table to cool. I knew that the lack of visible reaction from her did not mean she was unconcerned.

"Perhaps you could keep an eye out?" I ended, a little awkwardly.

Martha looked at the others, then nodded shortly to me.

I picked up Francis to spare Martha shooing him away from the cooling parkin and went up to the parlour to Gwendolyn, who was mending the fire. The room we used as a parlour was really the old chapter house, which the monkish hierarchy had used for meetings, and was now an outlandish but not charmless mixture of medieval, Tudor, Queen Anne and Regency furnishings—every era, in fact, in which the Worms family had had any money to buy things, which they certainly did not have at present.

Gwendolyn looked so happy just then that I hated to tell her about the possible intruder, but tell her I must. She would know far more about how to defend the place from dragon hunters than I did. I savoured the contented expression on her face for a moment before I spoke.

"Gwen, I've got some bad news, I'm afraid."

She looked up. "My sisters?" There was an edge to her voice. How quickly her mind leapt to disaster!

"They are very well, and looking forward to seeing you soon," I reassured her. Her younger sisters Violet and Una were staying with my parents in the East Midlands and would be here to spend the summer months with us at the Abbey in a few weeks. "I found some evidence of a stranger in the Dale today."

I relayed to her exactly what I had seen and what I suspected. Lily came in with the tea tray while we were talking.

"I suppose it might be nothing but a peddler," I said doubtfully. At that moment Lily turned sharply and upset a tea cup with her elbow. It smashed on the floor near the hearth.

"I'm very sorry, ma'am," she said to Gwendolyn, bending to clean up the pieces.

Gwendolyn shook her head kindly.

"Never mind, Lily. Strangers set us all on edge here at the Abbey, don't they? Don't hurt yourself."

Lily nodded, her eyes on the carpet. I was surprised to see her hands tremble a little as she picked up the shards.

"No, it won't be a peddler," said Gwendolyn. "A peddler would have come to the house to try and sell his wares, not hidden himself in a barn, if a peddler ever did find his way out here."

She was right.

"What ought we to do?"

"I shall tell Thomas to clean Father's gun, and to keep it loaded, and I will ask Dugdale to arm himself as well," said Gwendolyn.

"But Gwen—ought we really to shoot someone? I mean, Rivers died, but that was his own fault. We didn't kill him."

"Edith, anyone who would come here secretly...don't you think they would be willing to do violence? Do I need to remind you of what Rivers attempted to do while he was here?"

I felt myself go pale. Rivers had been willing to cause my brother's death.

"We must warn them at Drake Hall, also," she said. "I shall send a message by Pip."

"Let's not send him alone, not now," I said quickly. The hidden valley suddenly felt less safe amongst this talk of strangers and guns, and it would soon be evening. "It's my visit to Mrs Drake tomorrow. I'll tell them."

Gwendolyn looked at me, and her expression was enigmatic. "You're there all the time these days. What is it you find to talk about—Marsi secrets?"

"Mrs Drake likes me to sit and read with her, mostly. She piques my curiosity."

"Oh?" There was a strained note in her voice. Surely she did not begrudge Helena my visits?

"She's always giving me little tidbits of family history, clues really, and making me work the rest out. It's a little like a detective story."

That brought to mind my manuscript. I cleared my throat to bring it up again.

"Well," said Gwendolyn before I could speak, "I'll be studying the circulatory system most of the day, anyway, so you'd be dull here with me. You'll think me odd, Edith, but it's so fascinating, ever so much better than a novel." Her face was happy again. I balked. She noticed.

"Oh, how silly of me!" She set her teacup down. "I forgot all about your novel! I am sorry, Edith."

"No, don't be, it's quite all right."

"Do you really think I'd be any good though? Won't you want someone more...literary than me?"

Oh. She thought my obvious nerves were due to my inexperience as a writer, when in reality I was a very successful author trying to reveal myself as such to a friend. While I was contemplating this misunderstanding (which was entirely my own fault), Gwendolyn had another idea.

"Oh! I know! Simon!" She brightened. "Simon is the perfect person to look over it for you. He's read ever so many more books than me—he'll tell you how to make it better."

Make it better! Well, I really had no right to the irritation I felt.

Gwendolyn's eyes were bright with mischief. "Anyway, Dr Jenner, it was your idea to inoculate him. Maybe you'll manage to irritate him at last."

Irritate him! This was quickly going from bad to worse.

"Never mind, Gwendolyn, I think I'll forget about it for a while."

"Oh. Yes. If you like. Of course, if you really want me to read it—"

"No. I don't think I do, after all," I said, and it was true.

I got Gwendolyn to talk about anatomy for a while as I soothed my wounded pride with gingerbread. She paused after a while, looking at me thoughtfully, her brow crinkling.

"Your hair, Edith..."

"Sorry, it must look a fright after my run through the rain." I reached up a hand to pat at it.

"It looks absolutely lovely."

"Oh!" I exclaimed with pleasure. "That was Helena's maid. Does it suit me?"

"Very much." She was still scrutinising me.

"Do be careful, won't you?" She said softly. "At Drake Hall?" Her eyes were full of concern for me. It warmed my heart.

"I certainly shall. I have no wish to meet anyone else remotely like Rivers." I felt a chill when I remembered the ashes of the cooking fire in the barn. I could not imagine Rivers living in hiding; concealing himself in the outbuildings and the woods. This man, whoever he was, had been used to a different life. In fact, he might be far more dangerous. "I think I'll take Francis with me tomorrow. He's bitten for me before."

As I was readying myself for bed, I was startled to glimpse myself in the mirror. I touched my hair in surprise. With it twisted into a low chignon at my neck, I really did look different. And there was no orange fluff springing up about my face like a dandelion bloom gone to seed—instead, the hair around my face had gracefully formed into distinct curls.

Who was this girl in the mirror? I no longer recognised her. Perhaps the enchantment I had sensed at Drake Hall had been real, in some way. Perhaps I was becoming a character from a fairy tale, instead of everyday Edith, the slightly starchy clergyman's daughter.

I put down my hairbrush. I had brushed my hair religiously every night since I was twelve. I felt a creeping sense of guilt for not brushing it now. I shut the hairbrush in the drawer to get it out of sight. Then I took the pins out and, not having a comb like Helena's, raked through the curls as best I could with my fingers. Then I plaited it and went to bed.

In the morning I arranged my hair as much as possible as the Drake's maid had done the day before. Somehow, this felt like part of my new role as a protector of Ormdale. I felt as if I'd gained half an inch of height at least.

Francis swam about in the washing water in the basin on my dresser, nimbly steering in a tight circle with his tail. His yellow markings were very bright this morning. I felt a fierce burning in my breast at the thought of someone trying to take him from me.

After breakfast I put him on a lead. He was still small enough to perch on my shoulder but I wanted to accustom him to it before he grew much bigger (Helena told me his kind could grow as long as a man is tall). And with a stranger loose in the Dale, I wanted to keep him close.

I went down to the kitchen, planning to take a tidbit for him in case he became stubborn on the way and I had to coax him. I found a bit of parkin in the larder and put it in the pocket of my mackintosh.

While in the kitchen my eyes chanced upon the knife in the leather sheath that I had carried with me on my first dragon adventure. Impulsively, I picked it up. Gwendolyn had told me it was of great antiquity. Gripping it, I almost sensed in it some kind of mystical power—I felt instantly emboldened to confront all manner of dragon hunters.

"Let's go, Francis," I said.

I took the shortest possible route to the Hall. Francis stopped every now and then to look about us for a moment, his thin forked blue tongue flicking in and out. Was he sensing a stranger in the Dale? Or just looking for a mate?

I was not sure if there were any more of his kind. I had unintentionally hatched him myself by putting him in the fire in my study. I wondered how long he had slept cold and alone in his egg in that log, waiting to be woken by fire. I felt a pang of sadness that he might look in vain for a counterpart.

Once arrived at the Hall, I breathed a sigh of relief. I wasn't sure how Mr Darcy would feel about Francis, so I tied him up in the walled garden at the back of the Hall, near the sundial, where he seemed quite happy to hunt insects, hiding in the bushes and then leaping out at them. Would he try to eat any of the dragon-birds I had seen on my last visit? Or would that be a kind of cannibalism? I would have to ask my brother when he arrived in a few weeks.

I almost ran into Simon in the dim hallway. I told him quickly about my suspicions of an intruder. He listened gravely.

"And now Gwendolyn's getting Thomas to clean the guns," I finished.

"That troubles you?"

I nodded.

"I'll take Pilot and have a look around. Perhaps we may deter this intruder by a show of watchfulness."

"Thank you," I breathed.

He was already putting on his coat. "Edith."

"Yes?"

"Would you mind not telling my mother about this, yet? I'll do it myself, once we know more."

"Of course."

I went upstairs. Once again, I paused on the threshold of the room.

"Edith?" came the voice from inside. I opened the door and went in. The carpeted stillness of the room took me into its hushed embrace.

"Good morning, ma'am," I said, seating myself.

"You are a little early," she said, with a smile. Today, her gown was the colour of a garnet, which made her hair appear brighter.

"How do you tell?" I asked. "The clocks..."

"Ah," she said. "I suppose it is the light." The light from the window was scant. I was impressed.

"I do hope that extra-sensory perception is part of being a Marsi," I said longingly. "I know a sense of direction isn't, since I have none. I only find my way around the valley because of the admirably well-marked paths your son maintains."

She laughed. It was a silvery sound. Then she went quiet.

"I'm not certain what is me, and what is Marsi. Before you came, I had never met another like me," she confessed.

I was astounded.

"But surely there were others in the family? Gwendolyn told me there were."

"I suspect that it is only heritable if two bloodlines meet with the capability of producing Marsi. Before my time, there had not been another Marsi here since the Regency."

"But that was a hundred years ago!" I exclaimed.

"Indeed."

"Then we are as rare as...as dragons."

"Rather rarer, I should think."

I realised she was right. I had seen half a dozen dragons in the Dale so far, and only two of us. Yesterday I had fancied myself becoming a character from a fairy tale. Now I discovered I already was one.

"So you see now why you are a kind of miracle to us," she said. "And why I pray every day that you stay." Her eyes met mine. They were such an uncommon grey. There was a vulnerability in them I had never seen there before.

Helena's question about my intentions toward Simon now appeared in a different light. Was it possible she hoped that more Marsi might be produced by combining our bloodlines? This made me feel almost ill. Perhaps it wasn't entirely rational of me, but to think of Simon and myself as a *breeding pair* (as one would a fine brood mare and a stud) filled me with repugnance.

Helena must have sensed that I was troubled by her words, because she went on.

"When your uncle died, Edith, I prayed for someone who could give this family what it needs." Her voice was low and quiet yet it had more emotion in it than I had ever heard there. "For years I was forced to rely on his extremely dubious judgement. Restricted to my own chamber, I could only advise. He was a very vexatious man to advise." She laughed, but it was a despairing laugh. "He despised women, you know. I think he only asked my advice so he could do exactly the opposite of whatever I recommended. I had to constantly urge him towards the most idiotic courses of action, simply so that he would act in opposition to me."

"How exhausting," I said, appalled to imagine it.

"It was. And as my illness worsened, I began to despair. But then you came."

For the first time since I had met her, I felt I was seeing beneath the mask of queenly control. She reached out her hand to me now and I took it; there was an urgency in her grasp that flattered me.

"The men have had their way in Ormdale for generations. Now it's our turn, Edith. Simon is very good, but he has no will to rule. Your father is the same, I think. Gwendolyn has a kind of strength, and I thought for a time that she would be the one, but she suffered too much under her father's reign. She is too easily influenced, too fearful. But you—it's not only that you are a Marsi. You are different."

Was it my imagination or was her hand trembling slightly in mine? My head was spinning as I strove to take in this extraordinary conversation. Her words made me feel strangely elated.

"How—how am I different?" I asked.

"You have ambition. You have energy. You can see things not as they are, but as they could be. As I do." I gripped her hand back. "I see this family becoming strong again. What do you see, Edith?"

I reflected. What did I see? What did I want, for this complex new family of mine?

Suddenly my head cleared, and I knew.

I wanted to clean the rotten part of Ormdale—that thread of manipulation that kept people here from a sense of duty and loyalty and seemed to drain them of their real purpose.

I wanted those who stayed to stay out of love, because there was beauty here, too, and beautiful things that were worthy of protection. Surely, that would be true strength.

"I see that, too," I agreed with her.

The expression on her face was a kind of relief; as if a long-threatening cloud had lifted. She gave my hand a gentle pressure, then removed it to smooth the bed-clothes, her customary serenity restored.

"Then we shall manage it together."

It was almost a question. But not quite. She said it as if everything was settled between us. I wanted to let it go, wanted her to keep confiding in me like this and treating me as an equal.

But I couldn't. Something rather important had not been settled. I swallowed.

"Why does it need to be managed?" I asked.

She looked at me, one eyebrow raised.

"I don't think— I don't agree that it needs to be *managed*, in that way. I don't think Gwendolyn and Simon and the others need to be ruled. Advised, yes. But not ruled."

"One cannot trust people to make the right decisions on their own, Edith," she warned.

"Not entirely on their own. We can bear each others' burdens, of course. But who am I to dispense decisions that others should make?"

"We make decisions for children every day," she said quickly.

"Gwen and Simon are not children!" I protested.

"But that's precisely what they are." There was a slight hardness to her voice now. "They were raised to remain children their whole lives. They don't even dream of a life without leading strings."

"There you are quite wrong, ma'am. Gwendolyn has dreams of a life, a new and different life, and she is pursuing it with hard work and determination. As for Simon, if what you say is true, then it is high time the leading strings were cut. And you are much the best person to do it."

There was silence for an instant. Then she laughed lightly.

"What a little revolutionary you are. You'll be hiding a knife in your toga next, I expect, to stab me with, all in the cause of freedom." She said it so mockingly that I felt I had made a fool of myself. I'm sure my cheeks grew red.

"No fear of that, ma'am. Unless you turn tyrant, I will have no need to play Brutus."

I met her searching gaze without looking away, though I was almost trembling myself.

In the end it was she who looked away first. "I find this conversation has tired me a little. Shall we read?"

I murmured an indistinct apology and automatically picked up my book when she did. She leaned back in her bed. I found myself worrying that our conversation might have harmed her. I glanced at her. She was reading a volume of Dickens. Her face was smooth and untroubled.

It was almost possible to forget the moment when she had offered me co-regency over our families as if it were some sort of magical power that was hers to convey.

But I didn't forget it.

Chapter Six

I retrieved Francis and left the Hall. I swung upriver to quickly check on the river-dragon's nest.

I soon saw that there had been a disturbance of some kind on the river bank. Heart thudding, I drew closer than I had yet dared to the nest itself and carefully pushed back the vegetation with my walking stick. Only one egg remained, bigger than a goose egg, faintly speckled with blue.

I breathed quickly and thought faster. There was a messy track as if someone had stumbled through the undergrowth. Perhaps the river dragon had encountered the hunter?

I turned and followed the tracks down river, moving as quickly as I could with Francis on his lead.

I was just considering that I had better go back to the Hall for help in case the intruder was close when I heard a shout on the other side of the river. I picked up Francis and ran towards it.

DRAKE HALL

Hearing more voices—were they children's voices?—I burst though a thicket of bushes and then stopped dead at the startling tableau which greeted my eyes.

Three children had their backs to me, looking at something in the grass at their feet. Two girls—one fair, one brown-haired—and a boy, who was holding a knotted tree limb, upraised, like a weapon.

"George! What on earth—" I gasped. The three of them spun round to face me.

My brother George's schoolboy face was tight with worry, his freckles standing out against his pale skin. He lowered the tree limb from attack position when he saw me.

"Is he dead?" said my cousin Violet, the older and browner of the two girls, in a tone of curiosity, pointing down into the grass.

"Is who dead?" I demanded.

They moved aside and I saw what they had all been staring at.

It was a man. He was lying unconscious in the grass. Next to him was a knapsack which was unfastened, and within it could be clearly seen five blue-flecked eggs, nestled carefully in sawdust.

"Good heavens," I exclaimed. "Did you whack him with that great branch?"

George nodded. "Violet told me to," he said, a little plaintively.

Setting Francis down on the grass behind me, I cautiously leaned over and checked the man's pulse. He smelled strongly of wood-smoke, hay, and rain. This was surely the intruder we had been looking for.

"It's all right, he's just unconscious. Well, children," I said, sitting back on my heels. "I think you've caught yourselves a dragon hunter."

Una, my youngest cousin, was hanging on to Violet's pinafore. Violet looked pleased. George looked sick. Una's blue eyes were even more enormous than usual.

"All right, you can tell me all about it later, including how on earth you got to be here, but right now you'd better go get help before he wakes up. I'll stay here and guard him. Girls, you run back and fetch Dugdale at the Abbey Lodge, it's not far. George, go on to Drake Hall. If Mr Drake is out, bring Forrester and any other men who are about. Quickly, now!"

The girls ran off. George started off, then turned back. "Shall you be all right here, Eddie?"

"Yes. I've got Francis. He's defended me before." I smiled a tight smile at him and pulled out the knife from its sheath. "And I've got this."

He nodded and disappeared behind the trees.

I was now alone with the unconscious dragon hunter. I thought about searching his pockets but I couldn't bear the idea of him waking up and seizing me while I was doing so. I contented myself with scrutinising him from a safe distance while I waited for reinforcements.

He seemed a little below medium height and not particularly well-nourished. His worn factory-made clothes marked him as urban poor; the class of person I had occasionally (reluctantly) visited when assisting Mother with her charitable work in the parish. I had a sort of feeling that he might be foreign. I guessed he was in his early thirties.

But by far the most striking thing about him was that the skin on almost half of his face was pitted and ridged with scar tissue. This disfigurement spread over his left ear and cheek, with an area that was less effected around his eye. I saw that the back of his left hand was also identically marred. It looked as if he had been burned in an explosion, and had saved his eye from injury with his hand. Certainly, he was nothing like the well-fed and self-satisfied Rivers.

He began to stir faintly. I looked about me but could see no signs of approaching reinforcements. I held my knife as threateningly as I knew how and stepped back so Francis was between us.

He didn't see me at first, and made a motion of grasping about for his knapsack.

"If you are looking for what you stole, it is here," I said.

He startled and looked at me. His body went still and tense when he saw the knife. The knapsack still lay open on the ground. I stepped in front of it.

"Before you think of assaulting me, I should warn you that this creature has been trained to defend me and is possessed of a deadly venom."

His eyes flicked back and forth between the knife and Francis. Francis did not seem to have realised this man was a threat and was basking in the sun and looking particularly small. I pondered writing down an observation on my notebook page as follows: '*Varanus salvator*' — *basks uselessly in threatening situations.*

I sensed that I needed to expand on the situation to intimidate him.

"My friends are on the way, strong men who will not take kindly to any offence to myself."

I knew immediately this was a misstep as it betrayed my own vulnerability. I certainly had no real intention of stabbing him, and in strength and desperation I must be his inferior. I felt by the way his eyes were assessing me, his body tense and ready to spring, that he was weighing up his chances of grabbing his loot and making an escape before help arrived.

Perhaps if I could keep his interest, I might distract him long enough to make escape impossible.

"I should tell you, this is no ordinary knife," I announced. "This knife was given to my family by King Henry. It has defended us for centuries."

His eyes narrowed a little, whether in doubt or interest I could not tell, but at least I was distracting him from running. I went on talking nonsense, trying to keep my voice low and, I hoped, formidable.

"You have seen that this valley is full of mythical beasts. We are a fierce and ancient race of dragon keepers here. You see even our children are a match for you."

I think at this point he decided I was quite mad. He slowly supported himself behind him on his hands. I was sure he was getting ready to spring. I let my voice rise to a pitch I hope sounded like a prophetess of doom, and not a lunatic.

"Beware! You have offended the River Dragon by stealing her children!"

At this point I sensed a swell of movement in the river. I had my back to it and didn't dare turn away from him. The man's eyes fixed on the river, wide with horror.

There was a slick sound of something large surging onto the riverbank, not far from me. I felt droplets hit my skirts.

I looked.

A large, mottled blue reptile the size of an alligator with aquatic fins and a very long snout made an indignant honking sound at us. Then it carefully scooped the eggs from the knapsack, holding them gingerly in its jaws, and slid back into the water.

We both stared after it.

The man muttered a sentence in a tongue of the Slavs. I was quite sure it was not the kind of thing I would care to hear translated.

There was now a tumult as Dugdale and Thomas came crashing though the undergrowth from one direction, and Forrester and a groom and stablehand from Drake Hall appeared from the other.

I lowered and sheathed the knife in relief. George appeared at my side.

Dugdale was asking me where the man should be taken.

I looked at him in confusion. "We must question him, mustn't we?"

Dugdale nodded. "I'll put him in the holding cells below, Miss."

This was beginning to seem worryingly lawless.

"Ought we to send for someone? I don't suppose there are police anywhere closer than Embsay?"

"Not even there, but there's the magistrate here in the Dale," offered Dugdale.

"Oh, yes, of course, please send for the magistrate," I said, much relieved. I couldn't remember if I'd met the magistrate, but I had a dim recollection that I might have.

A look passed from Dugdale to Forrester. Forrester nodded and slipped away while the other two men from Drake Hall fell in with us to lend assistance.

We then began an awkward procession to the abbey, with Dugdale and Thomas on either side of the man, holding firmly to his arms, and George, Francis, and I following behind.

The longer I watched our captive the more my natural antagonism waned. He was undoubtedly a poor thief in the employ of some malignant mastermind who yet lurked in the shadows. His disfigurement, which had inspired momentary revulsion, now influenced me to pity him.

I wondered if he even understood English. I rather hoped he didn't, given all of the absurd things I had said to him.

I was able to question George now and discover that Mother and the children had decided to begin their Yorkshire holiday early. Apparently, it had been unseasonably hot in town and there were concerns about an outbreak of influenza. They had written to me but must have travelled in advance of their letter.

The three children had set out to find me but instead had come across the stranger and witnessed him stealing dragon eggs on the riverbank. The river dragon had made a brief assay at him and he had run away from it and lost it in the bushes. Advised by Violet, the children had run further down the river path and lain in wait for him, then clobbered him over the head as he stumbled past them.

"Well done, George," I said.

"Thanks, Eddie. But what will Mother say?" he looked a little worried.

I merely gave his arm a squeeze.

Chapter Seven

Once at the Abbey, I deposited George with Mother and the girls and followed the men into the holding cells.

They had locked him in the cell only recently vacated by the wyvern.

I stood on my tiptoes to look through the opening in the door. He was sitting on the fresh bale of hay we had placed in the cell, ready for its next dragon occupant.

"Have you begun questioning him yet?" I asked Dugdale, who had settled himself on a crate.

"No, Miss. Reckon we'll wait for magistrate. That'll be him now."

The figure that came down the stairs was Simon.

"Oh, Simon, we thought you were the magistrate come to help us," I said.

"I am the magistrate," he said simply.

I was more surprised than I should have been. Perhaps I too, had unconsciously judged him as less capable than he was. Then

I felt a little displeasure. I had pictured in my mind some beefy squire coming to bluster and intimidate the intruder. I did not care to see Simon in that role.

Dugdale unlocked the cell door and Simon went in, leaving it open behind him so I had a clear view inside.

The man looked up at Simon without moving. Simon sat down on a small stool and looked at him. Neither of them said a word.

"I know who you are," said Simon at last.

The man startled at this and narrowed his eyes. Finally, he spoke.

"I find that hard to believe, since I don't have any idea who you are." His voice was lightly accented, but from his choice of words it was clear he was well-versed in the English language.

Simon let another moment of silence go past.

"I don't know your name. I suspect you are a skilled worker who has lost work because of an accident. Someone paid you to come here and steal from us. But I think you mean us no harm. I don't think being a thief is satisfactory to you. You are hungry now?"

The man swallowed. He looked at the floor. It was clear he had no hope of any food being offered to him.

Simon glanced at me.

"I'll fetch some tea," I said. I moved away, but not too quickly to see the intense surprise on the thief's face.

As I went upstairs, I said to myself that if Helena Drake thought her son was still a child, she was entirely wrong.

I sent Lily down with a tray. She seemed a little indignant when I explained who it was for, but her expression quickly returned to its usual stoicism and she laid out the plain kitchen crockery and a thick slice of bread and butter.

"A strong cup of tea, I think, with sugar," I asked. She obeyed, though I noticed she stinted a bit on the sugar.

I went up to see Mother.

The children were reenacting their moment of triumph for her in the sitting room. She herself had been pressed into the role of the thief and George was brandishing the fireplace poker at the critical moment when I came in. I sat down and watched.

Mother crumpled to the floor with a satisfyingly theatrical gasp. I was impressed but not surprised. Mother had always rather excelled at theatrical games.

At that moment, Gwendolyn came in the room. She paused in the doorway, taking in Mother on the carpet and George with the upraised poker and Una clinging to Violet's pinafore.

"I see you've made yourselves at home," she said.

Then she held out her arms to her sisters. They went to her embrace eagerly. It was the first time I'd seen them show such open affection to each other and it warmed my heart.

I looked at Mother meaningfully and gave her a nod which meant *Well done*. She smiled back at me in a way that said *You, too*.

She got up, shook her skirts into place, and came to give me a kiss of greeting on the cheek.

"Any news of the prisoner?" Gwendolyn asked me.

"Simon and Dugdale are still with him," I answered.

"Yes, I heard that he had tea," Gwendolyn said crisply. I gathered that Lily must have complained about it to her. "I think it's almost time for ours."

"Let's sit, children," said Mother.

While we waited for the arrival of the tea tray, the children begged me to tell my part of the story. They were most impressed by my wild threats on the riverbank. When I got to the part about the knife, Gwendolyn made a sound of mingled amusement and exasperation.

"Edith, you've such an imagination. It's no wonder you write."

"But Gwendolyn," I objected, finding this unfair, "It was you who told me about the knife."

Gwendolyn blinked rapidly.

"Gwendolyn?" I asked.

"Oh, well, I'm afraid I'm the one who made that up," she said briskly.

"What?" I exclaimed.

"You mean it's not a magical royal dragon knife?" asked George, disappointed. As I felt the same, I thought his reaction quite reasonable.

"I believe cook finds it magical for slicing onions. But I don't think it could be called royal in any sense," she said regretfully.

At that moment Lily came in, a little flustered, with a tea tray laden with hot pasties. As we began to dig into them she paused near the door.

"What is it, Lily?" asked Gwendolyn.

"It's mother's best kitchen knife, m'am. We can't find it, not nowhere. Do you suppose the stranger..." There was dread in her eyes.

"Oh," said Gwendolyn.

Everyone was looking at me. I swallowed my mouthful of tea rather fast.

"You'll find it in my mackintosh pocket, Lily. Please apologise from me to cook," I said with a brief glare at Gwendolyn. "It won't happen again now I know what it's really for."

As soon as she left the room we all fell about laughing. Mother stirred her tea serenely.

"Well, I see my children have been engaged in not just ambush and assault, but also theft. Perhaps it's the two of you who should be cooling your heels in one of those cells."

"Speaking of which," I said, sobering quickly, "I wonder how they are getting on down there."

"What are they going to do with him?" asked George.

"Hang him, most likely," said Violet, her mouth full of pasties.

Mother delivered a calm but quelling look. Violet swallowed and wiped her mouth daintily.

"Pardon," she said meekly. "Hang him, most likely," she repeated in a ladylike tone. I tried not to laugh. I liked Violet. I had thought her quite uneffected by the gothic air of the Abbey, but I now saw that I'd been wrong. The way she took doom and gloom quite in her stride, as the normal order of things, must be an effect of her upbringing.

"Don't be absurd," said Gwendolyn. "Of course we won't hang him."

But she didn't make a suggestion for what ought to be done with him, and I didn't want to ask in front of the children. What on earth *could* be done about him, after all?

Simon and Dugdale came in shortly after that. Mother took the children gracefully away while Gwendolyn poured the two men tea.

"Has he said who sent him?" I asked them straight away.

"He says only that it was a scientific gentleman, whom he was to meet in Regent's Park in three days time."

"And you believe him?"

"I believe that he was paid to come here, and that he has no personal interest in Ormdale and its peculiarities. Do you agree with me, Dugdale?"

"Aye," Alfred nodded.

"He had a job as an overseer in a dye factory," explained Simon. "There was an accident with the chemicals, which were being used improperly."

I shuddered. His face.

"His employers did not like to have him about the factory after that," Simon continued. "His appearance would not have a salutary effect upon the workers, I think."

Dugdale grunted. "I've seen the same at limeworks. Men who've been scarred or injured, sent away, so's not to discourage others."

"And you think to bring such a dangerous industry to Ormdale?" Gwendolyn asked, a little unexpectedly. The conversation seemed to have set her on edge a bit.

"Not the way I'd run it, ma'am," he said patiently.

"Never mind that now," I said, with considerably less patience. "The question is, what is to be done with the man?"

There was a moment of silence.

"If he is in such a desperate situation, then when we let him go, surely he will sell our secrets to this scientific gentleman?" Nobody disagreed with me. "We can't keep him underneath the Abbey indefinitely. And we can't let him go. So what can we do?"

Dugdale drank his tea, as if to underscore the fact that he did not have any idea.

"Perhaps," said Simon slowly, "We might do none of those things. Perhaps we might do something to improve his situation."

I stared at him. Then I sat up straight in my chair.

"That's it! We must give the man a job."

Chapter Eight

After Gwendolyn's horror had died down and Dugdale's doubts were expressed in blunt monosyllables, everyone started to feel that perhaps this wasn't quite as mad a scheme as it had seemed at first glance, though it certainly was not without possible drawbacks. Simon stayed fairly quiet but I suspected that he and I were of the same mind. It was agreed that we should all reconvene to make our decision the next day. We dispersed.

Simon went home, Dugdale went to his rooms in the Lodge, and Gwendolyn went off to soothe her scattered nerves with anatomy.

I sent Thomas down to our prisoner with some bedding and then I went up to Mother's room with Francis to spend the evening with her. I was eager to hear all her news. Parish tidbits would be a welcome distraction.

I found Mother steadily mending her way through a pile of socks which I would have happily consigned to the dustbin without a pang.

I sat with her, stroking Francis's speckled yellow belly, and forgot my own worries for a while in her charming descriptions of Violet and Una's introduction to life outside the Dale, and the familiar goings-on of Father's parish.

"What about you?" she inquired after a while, knotting a thread with slim, capable fingers. "You've had trickier business here than my workaday charity bazaars and orphan committees."

"Oh, no!" I disagreed. "I consider lonely wyverns and angry river dragons much easier to get on with than some of Father's parishioners. And as far as charity bazaars—well, you know how I feel about those. The longest afternoons of my life were spent standing in a stall, waiting for someone to decide which d'oyleys to buy, all of them hideous beyond belief. I felt my youth draining away, as if Stoker's vampire were taking it. I have the highest respect for your work, Mother, but I would not change with you. I am not brave enough for it."

She laughed and began darning a tremendous hole in one of George's socks. It was, I thought, more hole than sock.

"You seem to have made friends here," she noted.

"Yes, I think I have," I smiled. I was pleased at her noticing this, as I'd never shown much of a talent for making friends before. "Gwen and I get along very well.'

"I'm so pleased you told her about your writing."

My smile vanished.

"Edith?" Mother prodded. "You did tell her? She said—"

I hung my head like a child. "I only told her I'd written a manuscript of a novel."

"Oh, Edith."

"I tried, really I did, but I don't think she cared much about it."

"Edith," Mother set her darning down in her lap. "I know you've been a good friend to Gwendolyn. A marvellous friend. But you ought to let her be a good friend to you as well. She may not care much about it, but you do. It's not fair to her to pretend you don't."

I sighed. I felt she was right. Mother went back to darning. She was never one to press a point or demand agreement. Her darning needle flashed in the candlelight.

"And Simon," she mused, in an open-ended way.

"And Simon," I repeated, as neutrally as possible. Oh well, better have it out at once. "It's a bit of a bore," I said, "But I suspect he wants more than friendship."

"Is it a bore?" she asked mildly.

I looked at her quickly but she was darning as innocently as any person could darn.

"I sometimes think I shan't marry at all, Mother," I confessed.

"Do you? Why do you think that is?" she inquired, curious but totally unconcerned.

"Well, the writing for one thing. Most men seem to want one to…well…"

"Tend their stall at the charity bazaar?" Mother suggested, her voice a little wry.

"Yes, exactly! And I've just told you how that makes me feel."

"What about Simon? Does he have a charity bazaar stall that wants tending?"

I reflected on this. "I've no idea. He hasn't mentioned one."

"That could be a good sign, I suppose."

"Of course, you and father manage so well. I don't know how you do it," I said, with a touch of envy.

"It takes practise," Mother admitted. "But it helps if you want to play two parts of the same duet."

I looked at her quizzically. She paused in her darning.

"If you both want to play the same piece, you fight over it. And if you want to play quite different pieces of music, you lose each other a bit. But if you want to play two parts of a whole, you help each other, and you make something you couldn't have made, all on your own." She dimpled. "And of course, you must try very hard not to elbow one another while you are playing, though it *will* happen from time to time."

I thought about this.

"So I must find a man who wants to play a duet with me? But how do I know?"

"It helps if you are friends," she said gently. "It makes it ever so much easier to know."

"How did you manage it with Father?" I asked.

I had always suspected the driving force in their courtship had been Mother. Father was a very humble man. Having been disowned by his family for marrying my real mother, he had no family connections to advance his ecclesiastical career, and when she died leaving him an infant to raise alone, his future was very bleak. Emily Fairweather—sweet-natured, well-bred, and lovely, with a modest but helpful fortune of her own—had been the desired object of many suitors far bolder than George Worms.

"Well, as you know, he was a desperately poor curate, and I was a meek little village schoolteacher." Her lips worked as if suppressing a laugh. "And I needed a lot of help with the village's annual charity bazaar."

"No!" I exclaimed.

"Mm," she nodded. "Such a long afternoon it was. I believe our stall had pincushions, and an abundance of painted screens. But it flew past for us, we got along so well. And then I needed his help with reconciling the numbers after."

"You never did!" I almost howled with laughter.

Father was famously terrible with figures. Mother and I were the appointed bookkeepers in the family.

"And yet, I found I did," she said sweetly, picking up her work again.

"You reeled him in!" I accused.

"Hush. I never did." She wagged her thimble at me for emphasis. "Listen, a man like your father will brave anyone and anything in the cause of what's right. But to ask for something for himself, something that he alone wants and needs, ever so desperately... He wouldn't lift a finger. I simply made it terribly obvious that I wanted and needed him just as much as he needed me. And then—well, no one could stop him." Her face was glowing a little with the memory.

I treasured this story. But I hardly dared hope that I might share my life with someone as congenially as did my parents. One thing I was sure of: I would never be able to do it with a man who would be embarrassed or dismissive or—God forbid!—*threatened* by my novel writing. And I suspected such a man would be hard to find.

"And now I want to ask you a favour," Mother broke in to my reverie.

"Yes?"

"It's Una."

"And what can I do for Una, pray tell, that you cannot do far better, Mother?"

"Be yourself—be our own resourceful and loyal Edith."

I didn't mention that being myself was becoming rapidly more complex these days, with so many new parts being offered me to play. Instead I asked, "But why, Mother? Why does Una need an Edith, so particularly?"

"Because she's afraid," she said this very abruptly, and it chilled me a little. "I rather think she is afraid all the time. I'm not sure if she knows anything else."

"I should think Violet has courage enough for both of them," I laughed, remembering how she had led the charge upon the intruder.

"No. Violet is reckless," Mother said very firmly. "She hasn't a healthy sense of danger. That isn't courage, as I'm sure you know. Courage is going into a cave even though it frightens you because someone more frightened than you is trapped inside." She looked at me seriously. "Courage is love defying fear. And that's what those girls need."

"How on earth can I—"

"I already told you. Just keep being Edith, and take them along with you sometimes. What you are doing here—being a friend to Gwendolyn and Simon, and heaven knows what else you've taken on in this place—is courageous. And they will see it, if you let them."

I nodded, though I felt more than a little daunted at having Una to think of as well as everything else.

The next morning I went down to the cells early, with Mother's words about courage fresh in my mind. If I was going to advocate for hiring this man, I thought I ought to at least talk to him myself. I took Francis with me, and a leftover pasty I found in the larder.

I coughed outside the cell door to alert him to my presence. I heard a rustle within.

"It's me. Miss Worms," I called out.

There was a pause.

"The fierce dragon keeper?" came the response.

"Ah. Yes. That's me." I was slightly embarrassed, but I wouldn't let that deter me. "I have something for you."

I offered the pasty through the cell window, wrapped in a napkin. It was taken, wordlessly. Then I heard the rustling of him settling in the hay again.

"I'd like to open the door. Will you promise not to try and escape?"

Another pause.

"On my word as an English gentleman?" the voice asked, very dryly.

"I don't mind what you swear on. You're from the Russias?" I mentally groped for something sacred to Russians. "Could you promise on the honour of the Czar, or your Holy Patriarch, or something?"

There was a pregnant silence.

"I could. But since I am a Pole and a Jew, I could hardly be expected to keep it."

I could tell by his voice that he was laughing. And also that he was eating the pasty.

I almost laughed myself at that. And then I said something without thinking.

"My mother was a Jew."

The eating sounds stopped abruptly. Good heavens, why on earth had I told him that? It was something I hardly ever spoke of to anyone.

"Very well," he said at last. "I will swear on my mother that I will not try to escape. At least not this morning. This *kolache* is too good."

I slid the bolt and very slowly eased open the door.

He was sitting, Indian fashion, on the floor. The blankets behind him on the hay bale were neatly folded. He brushed pastry off his hands and nodded towards the black and yellow creature on my shoulder.

"I see you brought your venomous dragon."

"Yes. See here, I know I talked rot to you at the riverbank, but it was true about Francis. He is quite venomous."

The man looked from Francis back to me. I tried not to look at his scars, focusing instead on meeting his gaze.

"You also told me the River Dragon was angry at me," he said. "That, too, was true. Why have you come?"

"I wanted to meet you."

"We met."

"No, not like that. I want to know if you are to be trusted."

He stared at me. "You found me stealing."

"I know that. But I want to know if you are honest." I knew I was making a fool of myself, but I didn't much care, as I felt I was getting a measure of this man at the same time, which was why I had come.

"You mean, besides the dishonest part?" he asked. Again, his tone was as dry as toast.

I nodded.

"Oh, besides that I am very honest."

"All right, then," I said, a little awkwardly. "I shall go now."

He didn't react. I shuffled out with Francis.

"I'll send you another pasty," I said, and shut the door.

"Would you send me a book?" came his voice.

"Oh! Yes." I hadn't thought how dull it would be to be locked in there with nothing, but now that I did I felt awful for him. "What kind of book do you like?"

"Paine. Hegel. Engels. Marx."

"I'm afraid the library here is rather limited, especially when it comes to modern German philosophers," I said, regretfully. "I might be able to hunt out a Dickens for you, at a pinch. I suppose that's not really radical enough, though?"

I heard a snort. "Novels," he muttered scornfully.

"Right. Goodbye." I made my exit.

Drake Hall had an excellent library but the one at Wormwood Abbey, though admirable in its way, was full of fanciful bestiaries and arcane herbals.

I ran into Mother on the way to breakfast. "Oh, Mother, it's awfully dreary in the dungeons, so I'm looking for a book for our friend downstairs. Did you bring anything radical? And he'd rather it not be fiction, more's the pity."

Mother considered this, then brightened. "I've the perfect thing, leave it to me," she said.

It was so comforting having her about the place.

❧ · ◆ · ☙

After breakfast, Gwendolyn and I met Simon and Dugdale again in my study. We discussed what exactly we might be able to offer the prisoner by way of an olive branch. Gwendolyn was the most reluctant, but she was also the most persuadable person among us. I was reminded of Helena's words. *Easily influenced.* This made me determined to be more patient to bring out her views.

"Gwendolyn, if you think it would be best, or if you simply can't bear having him about the place at all, we can send the man on his way."

She fingered her watch. "You say he's not violent?"

"He could have overpowered me easily if he'd tried."

"Simon, you think this is the best way?" she asked.

"I think the man has suffered from ill fortune and we might try and see what an opportunity to alter that might do for him."

"Dugdale. What about you?"

Dugdale rubbed his bearded chin slowly.

"It seems to me most men do what'll profit 'em. If we send him away, t'only way he'd profit is by selling our secrets. If he stays, he profits by keeping them."

"Well, let's see what he says, then, shall we?"

I sent Thomas and Dugdale to fetch him.

He stood before us with a kind of lean nonchalance, but I fancied I could sense his tension like a coiled spring underneath it. Gwendolyn looked away for a moment when she saw his scarred face. I thought a slight look of contempt crossed his face at her reaction.

Simon addressed him. "We'd like to make you an offer."

The man's eyes narrowed slightly. "You want to pay me?"

"No," I said. "We don't bribe people not to steal from us. Our Saxon ancestors tried that. They paid the Dane-gold to the Vikings and as a result the Danes kept coming back and threatening them whenever they wanted more gold. They never got rid of them. They just got rid of their gold."

"Thank you for the history lesson. What is the offer?"

"You told me yesterday how you lost your job," said Simon. "Would you like to try another?"

There was a pause.

"What kind of job?"

"A better one than running from angry river dragons," I replied.

There was a flicker that might have turned into a smile, if he'd let it. Instead, he sat down and made himself comfortable in the chair across from us. I sensed Gwendolyn stiffen slightly beside me. We hadn't asked him to sit.

"I will tell you my name. It is Janushek. Brik Janushek."

Then he did smile, but whether it was because he'd annoyed my cousin and this warmed the cockles of his revolutionary heart, or for some other reason, I couldn't say. He had deep laugh lines, which went some way towards lightening the starkness of his scarred face. He leaned back in his chair.

"Now, Fierce Dragon Keepers...tell me about this job."

Chapter Nine

The next day was our regular day for getting letters. Today's batch included Mother's letter telling me she and the children were coming early, and a letter from my publisher's office, acknowledging receipt of my manuscript. It was also a day I usually visited Helena Drake. I felt a little ill at ease after our last meeting, and I was enjoying the Abbey being filled with people again. I didn't want to go, but I thought of Helena alone in her room and felt ashamed of myself. One awkward conversation should not be enough to put me off her entirely. I ought to make allowances for a woman who had spent a decade confined to her bedchamber.

I compromised by taking the children with me on my walk, mindful of Mother's request to include them as I went about my business. They could go exploring with Francis while I visited at the Hall.

"Can Pip come with us?" asked George hopefully.

"I don't see why not. Oh, on second thoughts we ought to ask his mother. She might be expecting his help."

The children ran off to get permission for Pip to join us. All of a sudden, I felt slightly uneasy in my conscience. I had seen Pip engaged in many tasks about the place. Why had I never questioned the morality of using a child as an unpaid servant? Oughtn't he to have the benefit of some schooling? In the event that the estate did ever go bankrupt, what would become of someone like him? I made a mental note to speak with Gwendolyn about this.

The children rejoined me with Pip, and the six of us—five humans and a dragon—set off. George and Pip took the lead with Francis.

"Will we see the Pole?" asked Violet, walking beside me, cheerful as usual. She had grown and I realised with a start that she was now close to my height.

"I don't think so. He's gone to live with Mr Dugdale at the Lodge and help him with his work."

"I know," said Violet. "The servants didn't want him in the Abbey. Lily is sleeping with a knife under her pillow,' she reported cheerfully.

"Oh, dear," I said. "I'm sure they'll get used to him in time."

"Cook says she doesn't know what a Pole eats."

"Violet, would you mind calling him Mr Janushek? I feel as if you are speaking of an object when you say 'the Pole'. And he seems to enjoy her good cooking as much as any of us do."

"We never call servants by 'mister'."

"Janushek, then. Now, Violet, you must tell me all about your life in town. Mother says she took you to see a light opera, one of my favourites, I believe."

"Oh! *The Pirates of Penzance.*"

We enjoyed our walk and conversation and I said goodbye to them at the door of Drake Hall, making sure to give Una an encouraging smile. I watched the girls' white pinafores through the foliage as they darted off, with Francis riding on George's cap. Oh, to be a child in this place, with a whole magical summer ahead!

As I walked in I was surprised to hear the sound of a piano. The music sounded like raindrops. Could Helena have managed to come downstairs and play for a little? I followed the sound, marvelling. I reached the room where the music was. The door stood ajar. I peered round it tentatively, not wanting to disturb the player.

A dark head and broad shoulders were bent over the keyboard like a great brooding bird. It was Simon. He was playing a Chopin piece I recognised, and playing it quite beautifully.

I must have made a sound because he turned round. I felt once again as if I had transgressed, watching him when he didn't know I was there. I really had to stop doing that.

Simon didn't seem to mind. He smiled his astonishingly sweet smile.

"Mother asked me to play for her," he said, sharing his delight with me at this request.

I ventured into the room. "I didn't know you played."

"Mother taught me, years ago. Before she was so ill. You?"

I touched the instrument. "A little. I've missed having one at the Abbey."

He took up a sheaf of music. "We used to play these together," he said softly.

Duets. It was a volume of duets.

"Would you..." he began.

Suddenly I felt my cheeks growing hot. "I should go up now." I turned to go, and then knew I'd been abominably rude. This was absurd of me. Simon knew nothing of my conversation with Mother. I turned back. "I do like Chopin. Perhaps we can play another time."

And then I escaped upstairs.

I could see something was very different the moment I entered the room, which made me forget my momentary embarrassment.

Helena was sitting up straighter than usual and her eyes were sharp. She held a folded paper in her hands. Mr Darcy had been ousted from his usual pride of place and was sulking at the end of the bed.

"Good morning," I said. "How well you look."

"Edith," she said. "I've something I must show you. It was delivered here.'

I was so startled at this greeting that I forgot the unpleasant aftertaste from our last meeting. She handed the folded letter to me. I saw now that it wasn't actually paper at all.

"Good heavens," I said. "Is this...vellum?"

She nodded. I unfolded it to read these unexpected words:

The Red Dragon will choose his bride
on Midsummer's Day.
Come to the Castle of the Winds
in Wild Walia
when the sun is at its highest
on eve of Midsummer's Eve.

My skin tingled. It was like a note from another world. But what world? I tried to keep my head by looking at it critically.

"Is it poetry? If it is, it's not very good. It sounds as if someone was trying to imitate *The Mabinogion*."

"I opened it before I saw that it was addressed not to me, but to Wormwood Abbey. But that's not the important part. It was directed to 'The Worm Warden.'"

"What?" I exclaimed.

"Yes."

I sat down with a thud. "What does Simon say?"

"I haven't shown it to him yet. I wanted to speak with you first. After all, it was sent to you."

I stared at her. "To me?"

"You are the Worm Warden now."

I realised with a shock that she was right. I had told myself I was finding my place, but it had found me. I was the Worm Warden. I shook myself slightly.

"But what does the message mean?" I turned the vellum every which way and even held it up to the light for secret messages.

"Is it a trick? Sent by the mystery man who employed Rivers and Janushek? Who else would know about us?"

She didn't answer. I lowered the vellum. I felt my skin start to tingle again. Helena's silences were always as important as her words.

"Ma'am? Does someone else know about us?"

Helena was looking down at the bedclothes. This was most uncharacteristic. I waited. She finally met my eyes and I saw that the grey was troubled, like a lake when the wind is coming up.

"There were others. Once."

I drew in a breath. "You mean....other Worm Wardens?" She nodded. "Why didn't I know of this?" I almost demanded.

"We've heard nothing of them for so long, that I came to believe they were more legend than fact. A month ago, did you even believe dragons ever existed?" she asked coolly. "In Ormdale we live in the narrow margin between truth and legend. It is not always easy to discern which is which."

"You're right," I admitted. "Please. Will you tell me what you remember? Anything at all?"

"Hand me my journal please." She indicated a book on her nightstand. I gave it to her and she opened it.

"I've written down, as best as I can recall, what I was told as a child. After I wrote it and read it back, it sounded like a fairy story. You may read it yourself." She passed me the book again. Her beautifully old-fashioned script enhanced the enchantment of the words:

A long time ago, we were entrusted with keeping England's dragons. The dragons needed to be kept because the common folk did not like them, for they preyed on their herds and flocks. They saw no good in them, and hired mercenaries to kill them. But dragons have many a time been the personal emblem of kings and queens, and monarchs and those who counselled them believed in their hearts that to utterly exterminate them would bode ill for their thrones and kingdoms. Five families of Wardens were given lands where dragons dwelt in caves, lakes, and rivers, though the age of the dragon slayers had reduced their numbers. They were to keep them secret and safe.

And so the Age of Dragons passed, though it was remembered in song and story. The glory and prestige of the Worm Wardens faded likewise, though among themselves they practised their arts with pride, and guarded their secrets jealously. In time, the families quarrelled or grew cold towards each other and diminished until some were forgotten entirely, though they had once been kin. Eventually, they fell so low that they were forgotten even by the kings and queens who had entrusted their living emblems to them. But they remained faithful, keeping watch; keeping England's dragons secret and safe.

And the world around them changed, and people were ashamed to think that their grandparents had ever believed in dragons.

Kings and queens...living emblems...these notes sounded answering chimes within me.

"That's what I missed!" I said at last, suddenly excited. "We're not just dragon keepers. We're *royal* dragon keepers. Henry gave us the Abbey, and Elizabeth gave you Drake Hall. The services rendered were to keep the dragons secret and safe. Elizabeth even chose a dragon as her personal emblem! They were important to her, for some reason. *We* were important to her."

I looked at Helena for confirmation.

Her lips had curved into a smile of approval, yet I thought her eyes were strangely regretful.

"Good child," she said.

I felt a warmth inside. Royal dragon keepers! Perhaps it ought to have overwhelmed me, but somehow, it all made me feel less alone. There were others, like us.

I looked at the vellum again. What an odd invitation it was, in every way. A drop of doubt fell with a sizzle on the warm place inside me.

"I suppose it's definitely about dragons, and not...something else?"

"Something else?" she repeated, somewhat blankly. "What else would it be about?"

"Nothing, of course," I said.

I dragged Simon back with me to the Abbey, found Gwendolyn, and spread the vellum on the table in front of them.

"Look. Just look."

Simon and Gwendolyn bent to examine it.

"It was addressed here, but accidentally put in the bag for Drake Hall," I explained quickly. "Now, what do you make of it?"

They stared at me, then each other.

"I never believed they existed," said Gwendolyn, a little pale, her voice tight.

"I always hoped..." Simon trailed off.

"*Hoped*?" repeated Gwendolyn in disbelief. "Hoped for what? More unfortunates trapped in places like this?"

Simon flushed. I looked at him, willing him to continue. "What did you hope?"

He spoke quietly and, I thought, to me only. "That there were people who knew more about dragons than we do."

I nodded, because I felt the same. But he went further.

"When I was younger, I wanted to train them," he said in a rush, and it sounded like a confession.

Gwendolyn made a sound. He turned to her now.

"They're intelligent, Gwen," he insisted. "As intelligent as horses, maybe more so." He turned back to me. "But my father wouldn't hear of it. Neither would my uncle."

"There's a saddle in the Muniments Room," I offered, almost breathlessly. "I'm certain it's not for a horse."

"I've seen it," said Simon quickly.

"Of course you have," I said. I was feeling all tingly again. Simon's dark eyes were somehow bright as they locked with mine. The embers of hope and wonder inside me felt like they were being fanned to a flame under his encouragement.

"What if these people aren't just keeping dragons..." he began.

"But breeding them!" I finished. I felt like we were thinking the same thoughts, racing together towards something that was waiting for the two of us to discover...

"Rubbish!" pronounced Gwendolyn.

We both looked at her. She jabbed a finger at the letter as if it offended her deeply. "What is this? Goat skin? Who sends goatskin letters? No one! Why? Because paper is superior! Everyone knows it is! 'I want to send a letter. Oh, first I must go kill a goat.' How ridiculous. And what's this "eve of midsummer's Eve?" We have a calendar now, with dates! Anyone who chooses to live in the past is either a phoney or an imbecile, and I want nothing to do with them." She sat down abruptly. I knew the best thing was to leave her to calm down on her own, so I bent towards Simon over the letter and spoke in a low tone.

"Do you think this message could be about dragon breeding? A dragon festival of some kind? Maybe the families used to meet for it. Maybe they want to start meeting again."

A resolve was shaping itself quickly within me. I felt as if I was on a train that was slowly gathering speed. The sense that Simon was on it with me added to the exhilaration.

"A Golden Age of dragons," he almost whispered.

At this Gwendolyn exploded. "There was no Golden Age! You know what there was? Unsanitary conditions! Death!

Plagues! I thank God I live at the beginning of the twentieth century and you should, too. I'm tired of people like you who want to live in the past."

We were silent for a moment. I tried to ignore the sting in her words. She was being unfair. I had chosen to be here to help her, not because I wanted to live in the past. She knew that. And now that I was here, how could I ignore the opportunity to meet more people like us?

I swallowed. I was now quite resolved on my course of action. "Well, now that I know how you feel, Gwen, I won't ask you to come with me," I said gently.

"Come with you?" Gwendolyn looked up.

"To wherever the Castle of the Winds is," I answered. "Because that's where I'll be two days before Midsummer. Around June 19th, I should think. That's in a month.'

Chapter Ten

It proved frustratingly hard to convince the other denizens of Wormwood Abbey of the potential benefits of my chosen quest.

Gwendolyn flatly refused to have anything to do with the discussion and buried herself in anatomy and Greek, declaring that *she* at least had no time for nonsense.

Mother seemed a little bewildered by my enthusiasm for rushing off into parts unknown to find a hidden stronghold of dragon keepers, and gently but firmly insisted we write to Father before any decision was reached.

Helena was cautious and uncommunicative about the whole affair, saying only that she thought it inadvisable for me to go alone. She was oddly insistent that Violet was the best person to accompany me, but did not explain her reasoning. As usual, I found her impossible to pin down.

There were two bright spots. Dugdale, while being singularly uninterested in the mysterious invitation, told me that he could run the sheep-clipping perfectly well without me (a relief, since I hadn't even known that midsummer *was* sheep-clipping time).

And, of course, Simon. I was delighted to discover that his passion for the subject equaled my own. He and I had both responded with immediate excitement to the possibility of another surviving family of dragon keepers. If my friendship with Gwendolyn was languishing as she vanished into her studies and scoffed at my interest in our family history, my friendship with Simon was growing quickly under the ascendant star of our shared interest.

I sent off my letter to Father explaining the invitation and my plan to attend and asking his opinion on the whole adventure. I had promised Mother that I would not make a final decision until I heard from him. So, when I wasn't finding ways to make the housekeeping expenditure more efficient, I took the children on rambles.

I threw myself into our summer of dragons. After all, the next best thing to actually being a child in this place—this 'narrow margin between truth and legend'—would be to spend my time with one.

We ate our lunch on top of the Great Rock and found a rowboat to mess about on the Orme, occasionally glimpsing a tantalising ripple of river dragon in its depths. I took *Treasure Island* with us and read aloud to them. When we weren't pirates, we lazed on our backs in the grass; but instead of gazing at clouds we spied out the glittering dragon-birds, fighting tiny duels in the sky.

Francis developed a startling habit of climbing trees and crouching there until he spotted something delicious in the undergrowth; at which point he would leap on it from above our heads, to the accompaniment of our screams of mixed delight and terror since we had long forgotten he was there.

We found the river dragon's new nest and checked it every day, carefully recording the number of incubation days. In doing this, George and I grew closer than ever before. Between us we made copious notes in the dragon notebook, and began to catalogue and organise the items in the Muniments Room on rainy days.

I grew to fully appreciate my brother's extraordinary memory for zoological details. It was like having an encyclopaedia of natural history with me at all times. He compared the dragons' habits to those of turtles, snakes, lizards—from creatures as common as domestic fowl to those as outlandish as duck-billed platypuses.

Violet and I got on as we always did—splendidly—but I didn't think I made much progress with Una. When she wasn't reading, sketching, or gardening with Mother, she attached herself wordlessly to Violet's pinafore; a witness to our adventures rather than a full participant.

And then there was Pip. He hung back, but in a different way than Una. He was much more conscious of the social divide than the other children were, and was careful to put himself last and ask for nothing. But with him I felt I did make progress. He had a natural talent for drawing, which George and I put to good use in our notebook. I sensed Pip expand under the encouragement, as if new possibilities were offering themselves to his young mind. I wondered if it was wrong of me to encourage him. How few possibilities there would be for him to improve his position in life.

At night, I dreamed of dragons I had never seen. Dragons as big as horses, with wings that stretched out in a curving arc of power. I even dreamed of galloping over the moor on the back of one, racing cloud shadows. I woke from the dream with my face streaked with tears of pure joy.

My imagination was gripped by the idea of riding a dragon. I would wait for Father's letter, but my promise to Mother did not mean I could not make any plans.

One day after tea, I slipped out in the lengthening evening to meet Simon at the library of Drake Hall.

When I arrived, he had already got a detailed map of England spread out for us to scrutinise. Francis prowled over it curiously. I nudged him away.

"It seems to me we have two significant clues," I began.

He nodded agreement.

"And I've found what one of them means," I said in triumph, drawing a book from my pocket. "It's the one about Wild Walia."

"It's Wales, isn't it?" he asked.

I gaped at him for a second. "Well, yes, but how did you—"

"The Red Dragon. The emblem of Wales. It's what I thought of instantly. And of course, 'Walia' isn't very far off," he acknowledged, a little apologetic.

"Of course," I said, recovering. "But I found where it's from, you see."

I opened *The Mabinogion* to the end of the final tale. Simon drew close.

"This is a Welsh mediaeval story about Taliesin, the bard," I explained.

"King Arthur's bard?"

"Yes, exactly. Taliesin gave a prophecy about Wales being conquered by the English—it's the final passage in the whole cycle of stories. Here, read it."

Simon read aloud. His voice was low and sonorous, the slight Yorkshire burr adding a pleasingly archaic quality. The words had set my skin tingling wildly the first time I read them and his reading did it again.

"A coiling serpent
Proud and merciless,
On her golden wings,
From Germany.
She will overrun
England and Scotland,
From Lychlyn sea-shore
To the Severn.
Then will the Brython

Be as prisoners,
By strangers swayed,
From Saxony.
Their Lord they will praise,
Their speech they will keep,
Their land they will lose,
Except wild Walia."

"It doesn't make one feel exactly ecstatic to be English, does it?" I remarked ruefully.

"Indeed. But Edith, all of their land has been lost—I mean, hasn't it?" he asked, seriously. "It says they will lose all of their land, except for Wild Walia. So the invitation is to a place that doesn't exist."

"But what if it does?" I almost whispered.

His brow furrowed. "Go on," he prompted.

"Think of it," I went on, trying to contain my excitement. "The Dale is like a world of its own. What if there's another place like it? Somewhere remote, and hidden, with its own ways and secrets, like Ormdale? But what if it's not English at all? What if it's really Wild Wales...just like the bard said it would be?"

I caught my lip and waited to see if he would tell me I was mad. Instead, he passed a hand over his hair in a distracted gesture of amazement. I smiled to myself to see his dark hair rumpled like a boy's. Then he looked back to me, and his face was very much a man's face, with a man's determination.

"All right, where do we look for Taliesin's Wild Wales?"

We both leaned over the map. He drew the candles closer.

"What about a valley? Something like the Dale..." I mused.

"No. The valleys are mined for coal in Wales."

I thrummed my fingers on the map.

"The mountains, then. Where would you hide the real Wales?"

Simon pointed to the Northwest.

"Snowdonia. Very mountainous. And I understand it's quite desolate."

"Any cover for dragons?"

"I think there are pine forests."

"Perfect."

I traced my finger over the mountains of Snowdon. Suddenly I stopped. It took me a moment before I could speak. I pinched Simon's cuff.

"Simon. It's there. It's right there."

His eyes followed my finger.

The Castle of the Winds.

It was on the map. I almost couldn't believe it.

I felt as if a window had opened and a breath of air from another world had come into the room, smelling of pine forests and snow. Our eyes met in the candlelight and we shared a look of mingled hope and excitement.

"We've found it. We've found the Red Dragon," I breathed.

After that there was much comparing of maps and railway routes to plan how we could best get to this remote place, and how long the journey might take. We were ridiculously elated with our discovery, and sharing it with each other was delightful.

"What do you think about the Golden Winged Serpent?" Simon said thoughtfully, when there was a lull in the excitement, and both of us had sunk into arm chairs to reflect. To my surprise, Francis had curled himself up on Simon's lap instead of mine. Simon stroked him now and then.

"The one that represents the Saxons—us, I suppose—in the prophecy? What about it?"

"Do you think it might mean that they know of—that they have—flying dragons?" The way he said it, as if he hardly dared to say it, made me pause.

"Well, if it comes to that, we have flying dragons here," I replied. "There's the dragon-birds. And the wyvern can fly a bit, can't it?"

"Only so far as a chicken can, if you allow for their relative scale. Just enough to get over a wall, really, to steal a lamb."

"What are you thinking, Simon?"

"I'm thinking that in the old stories, dragons flew. Large dragons."

"Topsell says in his book one flew over a city on the Continent in the fifteen-hundreds for three days, and everyone there saw it," I agreed. "It must have been very big indeed."

There was a pause again. He now had my entire attention.

"Simon, what are you really thinking?"

His eyes were so dark in the candlelight I couldn't see where the pupils ended and the irises began.

"Da Vinci sketched a flying machine for a man, and that German inventor was trying to perfect his when it killed him a few years ago. But what if we don't need a flying machine? What if we just need a flying animal big enough to hold a man?"

I caught my breath. I hadn't dared to tell anyone about my dreams of dragon riding. And here was Simon, a step further than me.

"Do you think me mad?" he asked.

"Only a little madder than I," was my response, accompanied by a shaky laugh. What a mad pair of dreamers we were!

All of a sudden I was acutely aware that I was alone after dark without a chaperone in the house of a single man of my own age who was only distantly related to me.

My face went hot. I covered it up by looking at my watch. "Oh, goodness. See what comes of visiting a house with no clocks striking in it. Mother will be wondering where I am."

"I'll walk you back," he said.

I allowed him to do so as far as the Abbey side of the river. We were quiet on the walk and I couldn't help feeling how pleasant it was that we seemed to be able to be quiet or talkative together with equal felicity.

"Simon, I want to say something," I said when it was time for us to part. "I was quite unkind to you in the past, before I knew you well. Once, particularly. When you and Gwendolyn asked me to take the oath. I feel I was unnecessarily harsh."

"You questioned my honour."

"Yes," I admitted, embarrassed.

"You were right," he said. "Don't regret your words. You spoke exactly as you ought. You always do."

"Now, that really *is* nonsense," I insisted.

"I'm afraid I behaved in a very unmanly way," he said. I heard shame in his voice, as it was now quite dark.

"Not at all, but...how was it that I upset you so deeply? I've wondered ever since."

"Because I'd been trying so hard to do my duty all my life. Mostly doing it not very well, but I prided myself on the effort, if nothing more. And then you asked why. Why? And I had absolutely no idea. The best answer I could find was that I'd been trying to do my duty solely out of fear of disappointing my parents. And that is perhaps a passable reason in a child, but not in a man. The irony of it hit me at that moment — that it only took one word from you to topple the structure. It was as flimsy as a castle made with toy blocks."

I understood. And I blamed myself for thinking him hysterical at the time. But there was something else I wanted to understand, before the opportunity passed.

"I think Gwendolyn felt the same. But...why don't you want to leave? Like Gwendolyn does? You heard what she said when I showed her the letter. She can't wait to leave this all behind and start again in London."

"Because, unlike Gwen, I believe that there are things here worth staying for," he said with a deep certainty.

My heart lifted. This was also what I had begun to believe, but he had put it into words.

Before I could tell him that, he added this, in a quieter, warmer tone: "And there are things here that I love."

I stepped back quickly. "Thank you for explaining," I said as calmly as I could over the thudding of my heart. "And thank you for helping me find Wild Wales. Goodnight!"

Clutching Francis, I turned and walked towards the lights of the Abbey, grateful that the darkness hid my flushed face, and reminding myself sternly that I did not have the time or the inclination for a love affair.

Chapter Eleven

I hadn't gone very far when I heard someone whistling not far from me in the darkness. I stopped in alarm. Would Simon hear me if I shouted for help? Would Francis defend me this time?

But wait, could the someone be whistling 'God Save the Queen'? This reassured me somehow.

"Who's there?" I called out.

"It's me. Janushek." He came a little closer.

"Why on earth were you whistling 'God Save the Queen?'"

"So as not to alarm you, Rusalka."

We had come now within the kitchen yard and I could just make him out in the light from the scullery. I could hear the dishes being cleaned there.

Janushek had his hands in his pockets and a slight smile on his face. He leaned against the wall of the kitchen yard.

"I thought to myself that any good Englishwoman would be relieved to hear that, when meeting a stranger in the dark."

I stared at him. "How thoughtful of you. And what were you doing, wandering about in the dark?"

"Alfred sent me to get some milk from the kitchen for the drink you call tea."

"The drink we call tea? Oh, I suppose you have it from a *samovar*, do you? And what on earth did you call me just now?"

"Rusalka."

"What does it mean?"

"It's a creature from our folk tales."

I felt a little unflattered and must have looked it.

"It lives in the rivers and when it goes on land it takes on the form of a beautiful maiden."

"Oh," I said, thoroughly mollified. "But why call me that?"

"It's what I thought you were, when first I saw you," he answered simply.

"You thought I was a *naiad*?" I said, in disbelief.

He shrugged. "I had just been chased by a dragon and knocked out from behind. The first thing I saw when I woke was a fierce young woman, towering over me and shouting at me, with hair like flames, standing between me and the eggs I had stolen. What should I think?"

I burst out laughing. "Well, then. Shall we go in and get the milk for the drink we call tea?"

He smiled and let me go first.

We walked through the scullery where Pip was scouring pots. I felt a twinge of guilt. Why hadn't I made time to speak with Gwendolyn about this yet?

"Hello, Pip," I said.

Just then Lily came into the scullery. She jerked back when she saw Janushek behind me. I decided then and there to take the bull by the horns.

"Lily, would you come and see me tomorrow in my study?" I said. She dipped her head. Now I'd really have to talk to Gwendolyn about Pip right away.

We continued to the kitchen. Francis jumped down to warm himself by the range. Cook and Thomas were sitting at the table. Thomas started to get up when he saw me.

"No, don't stand up, Thomas, I don't want to disturb you. Martha, Mr Janushek would like some milk to take to the Lodge."

No one moved. I blinked in surprise.

"Martha?"

Janushek made a move to go to the dairy. "I can get it myself."

Martha stood up.

"No. I'll 'ave no *offcumden* in ma dairy."

I waited while she stumped off and got a can of milk and thumped it onto the table. I had the distinct impression that had I not been there, this rudeness would have become outright hostility. I took a breath to quell my indignation. They must be given time to adjust to him, I reminded myself.

"Thank you, Martha. Good night, Mr Janushek, and thank you for walking with me. It was very dark out tonight."

"I am at your service, Rusalka."

Janushek made me a short but somehow irreverent bow and sauntered out with the milk. I sighed. He wasn't going to make it easy for them to accept him, was he?

On the way to my room, I saw Gwendolyn's light was still burning. I hesitated in the passage. I had been hoping for the *detente* between us to alter of itself over time. But now I really had to speak to her before I saw Lily. I knocked softly at her door.

"Yes, come in," she answered.

I went in a little timidly. Gwendolyn was in her nightgown, sitting on the bed with her books and notebooks open around her.

"Gwen, I've something regarding the household I need to speak with you about. But first I need to know something. Are you angry at me? I feel as if you are. And it's an awful feeling. Won't you give me a chance to apologise for whatever stupid thing I've said or done?"

She seemed to ponder this. I noticed that her eyes had dark hollows under them.

"The only thing you've said or done, Edith," she said slowly, "is to do something I was never able to do."

I sat down on the edge of her bed.

"But what is it?"

"You have found joy here."

She looked at me, and there was an apology in her eyes. "I'm sorry for being angry at you. I'm...jealous. And ashamed. That's all. You see, it's never been anything but...well, wormwood and gall for me here. All these years I thought I was bravely bearing up under a horrible burden, when really I just wasn't equal to the job."

I put my hand on her arm. "Don't say that. Say you weren't the right person for the job. You're equal to much more, I'm certain of it."

"But what if I'm not, Edith?" Her voice was small. There was that fear of failure again. Helena had said Gwendolyn had suffered under her father's sway, and I believed it.

"Gwendolyn, you're forgetting to eat and sleep because of..." I craned my neck to make out the text open in front of her. "*Peculiar Metacarpal Bones*. Really!" I pointed at the medical diagram. "This would be wormwood and gall to me, Gwen. You were made for this, that much is obvious."

Her face transformed with a smile of gratitude. "Thank you, Edith. You are such a good friend. I wish I could be a better one to you."

Again, I felt a stab of guilt. Mother had told me that by keeping such a big part of myself as my writing career from her, I wasn't giving Gwendolyn the chance to be my friend in return. But Gwendolyn had so much to worry about, ought I to really initiate her into yet another secret?

"Oughtn't you to try and get some sleep now?" I asked.

She nodded and shut her books. I helped her move them off the bed and then I tucked her in like a child. "What was it you wanted to talk about?" she asked.

I pushed away the insistent feeling that I should confide in her in return. Not now, of course not. She was so tired.

I spoke quickly. "It's about Pip. The thought of him has been troubling me a bit and I've realised why. I don't know why it took me so long to notice. It doesn't feel right to just use him as a servant. What do you think ought to be done for him?"

It took me a moment to realise the change that came over Gwendolyn's face. If she had seemed tired before, she looked wearied almost to death now. Her eyes went downwards, as if she was deeply ashamed of something.

"Oh," she said, her voice very low. "I'm sorry, Edith. I should have told you, I know. Are you angry with me?"

"Of course not!" I said in surprise.

"I just hated to speak of Father in that way, so soon after his death. It's all so sordid and small."

My stomach gave a lurch.

"You are right, of course," she said. "It doesn't seem right at all for Pip to be hauling wood and water, and all that, just as if he was only Lily's child."

Oh, dear heavens. Suddenly I was angry. Very angry. I tried to keep it out of my voice.

"Let's speak of it tomorrow," I said. "We're both tired. We'll think more clearly in the morning."

I kissed her forehead and went to my room, then I shut the door behind me and leaned against it. My elation from my meeting with Simon was now quite gone. I felt unbearably weary and frustrated. It seemed as if every time I got to the bottom of one secret in this house, another confronted me. And this one was the worst yet. There was no mystery here, only shame and injustice.

How angry I was at my uncle for taking advantage of a girl under his employ; a girl he must have watched grow up on the estate! A girl not much older than his own daughter!

I was angry at Gwendolyn for calling this horrible situation 'sordid and small' and for being more anxious about speaking ill of her father than mending the ill that he had done.

I was angry at myself for all the times I'd sat in my study and ordered Pip, my own blood-relative, to fetch things for me.

And finally, I was angry that I had not felt the full injustice of benefiting from a child's unpaid labour until I knew him to be related to me.

"God, help us," I said, and meant it.

Having slept hardly at all, I got up early and surprised Mother while she was still in her bedroom.

"Mother," I said right away, "if you do lessons with the children while you are here, would you mind having Pip with you too? He's rather good at drawing, by the way."

"How odd you should ask," she said, "I was thinking of that yesterday. I'm concerned he may have had little or no schooling, so I think it might be best to have him on his own at first, in case there's any difficulty with his reading, you know. I wouldn't want to show him up in front of the other children."

I gave her a fierce hug of relief.

"Edith, what on earth was that for?"

"It's for being your own dear self, and not having any horrible, horrible secrets," I said.

I went down to meet Lily. She was waiting in my study. She was a tall, statuesque young woman. I judged her to be a few years older than myself. Counting back, that would have made her about sixteen or seventeen when she became a mother. How wrong it felt for her to be waiting for orders from me. I represented the family that had used her so disgracefully. I soldiered on.

"Now, Lily, I wanted to talk to you about Pip. It occurred to me that as far as I can tell, he has never been paid for his work here."

"Miss?" she looked bewildered.

"I am now doing the books, as you know, with Dugdale, and I am quite aware that your pay is not enough to compensate you for the work that Pip does. It is hardly enough for your own. I am going to change that. I shall also see you receive an appropriate back-payment for his wages to date. However, I'd like to suggest that instead of keeping it you allow me to invest it for his future."

Lily's face was now shuttered and cautious.

"I realise this is a lot to take in, but I have something more to say. I should like to restrict Pip's working hours. Perhaps you can tell me how many hours you think he might be able to assist you and still have time for some schooling."

"Schooling?"

"This brings me to my third point. Would you give permission for Pip to join the other children at the Abbey for some lessons this summer?"

"Other children?"

"Yes. I'm speaking of my brother George, and my two younger cousins. My mother teaches them herself, as you know. It might not be the most *practical* education he could receive—Mother favours literature and drawing and nature study—but it will be something."

Lily was looking down now. Her hands were gripped tight together. If I had thought to expect pleasure or gratitude from her, I would have been disappointed. But in fact, I felt so ashamed for what had been done to her that I only felt grateful to her for not blasting me with righteous anger.

But perhaps I was rushing her. "Would you like to go away and think about what I've said before you give your answer?"

"No, Miss," she said, meeting my gaze with determination now. I felt that I saw before me the spirit of the tall and proud Danish settler from which she undoubtedly descended. Inwardly, I excoriated my uncle again. How *dared* he? "I've nowt to think on. My answer is yes."

Chapter Twelve

After this I needed desperately to get outside in the fresh air. I put on my mackintosh and went out with Francis.

I by no means considered the matter closed. Officially employing Pip was a very small step towards righting things, but it was a step I could make before I had a chance to consult with Father. As the Squire of Wormwood Abbey and now apparently Pip's actual uncle, he would be the best person to fully address the situation. I attempted to comfort myself with this thought. I would try and clear my head and think of more cheerful subjects.

I struck out across the now vacant sheep paddocks and soon found Janushek repairing one of the endless stone walls. A section had fallen away, as they frequently did.

Grateful for this distraction from my tortured thoughts about Lily, I decided to strike up a conversation.

"How are you getting on with Dugdale at the Lodge," I asked, after Janushek and I greeted each other.

"Alfred and I understand each other," he said, balancing a stone in his hands to assess its proper placement in the wall. Francis ran along the completed portion, looking for insects in the crannies.

"Indeed? Do you have much in common?" I asked doubtfully. I couldn't imagine what would link the stolid Dalesman with this interesting foreigner, whose personality seemed like quicksilver to me.

"Books," he said lightly, putting the stone in place.

I stared. "You don't mean to tell me Dugdale reads German radicals?"

"No, he reads English ones. Ruskin...Morris...Owen...and Mill," he placed an upright topstone as he said each name.

"Really?" I didn't try to disguise my surprise.

"Ah, you don't expect that from the lower classes."

"I don't expect it from Dugdale, at any rate. And he isn't 'the lower classes', you know. Not exactly."

"And you?"

"What about me?"

"What are you exactly?"

"I thought I was a naiad," I said, my lip trembling with laughter. "I'm not quite sure where I fit, as such."

He glanced at me penetratingly. "You speak the truth."

He was right. I had meant it as a joke, but today of all days I was feeling quite alien to this place and its hierarchies.

I sighed deeply. "I was raised in the middle class. But my father was desperately poor when I was a child, partly because of marrying my mother. No, we really were poor—don't laugh. We hardly had bread enough for the two of us at times. Then he married my stepmother and we were comfortable. Very comfortable. Until he inherited Wormwood Abbey, which puts us firmly in the landed gentry, where Father was born. And now that we belong to the upper classes we have to worry about money all the time, because it's very costly to keep up a place such as this, and we can't modernise in some ways that we might, because of this huge secret we all have to keep."

Janushek silently continued putting rocks in place. It felt like a metaphor for the estate. The walls fell down, and we rebuilt them, over and again. But we could never get ahead. Wherever we turned, there was always a pile of rocks, waiting to be reassembled.

"What about you?" I asked.

He raised his eyebrows.

"You are poor," I observed. "And you are clearly well educated. Where do you fit?"

He laughed and shook his head. "Don't you know? I'm a Jew," he said. "Jews don't fit. That's why people hate us."

I couldn't think of anything to say to that. I wondered if he intended to include me in that 'us.'

"Haven't you heard?" he went on. "'The wandering Jew.' They hate us because we don't stay where they put us." He placed a rock precariously to illustrate. "And when we want to stay put, when we want to stop wandering, and we have families, and we make something of ourselves, they make us leave. So we can wander again, and they can call us shifty...rootless." He knocked down the rock with the back of his hand and kicked it. He looked up at me with a smile, but it was an empty one.

I was starting to feel a little sick inside. Had people hated my mother that way? Had I myself been shielded from that hate only because I had the kind of name that hid my mixed blood?

"What do you say in English?" He took off his cap, as if that helped him think. "Ah, yes. 'Damned if you do, damned if you don't.'"

I watched him silently repair the wall. I wasn't sure how much more tragedy I could stomach today, but I had to ask.

"Were you forced to leave Poland? Your family..."

"Do you know the Russian word, *pogrom*?" he interrupted.

"No."

"It means 'to destroy.' It's a Russian word. You are Christian?"

Never before had I felt the slightest qualm at admitting it, but this conversation was taking an unsettling turn. "Yes."

"Remind me: what did Christ say to do to your neighbours?"

Here, at least, I felt myself on solid ground. "To love them as we love ourselves."

"Ah! The Russians have a different idea. Their *pogrom* is where you destroy your neighbours. Take their animals, their furniture, even their clothes. Burn their houses. Violate their women." His voice was light, but the words bit into me nonetheless. I knew as he spoke that these were not mere anecdotes, but things he had seen with his own eyes.

"Please—" I suddenly felt I couldn't bear to hear anymore. Certainly, I was near losing my composure.

"As long as your neighbours are from the same race as Christ himself, the priest will bless it all," he went on, his voice horribly calm.

My eyes were suddenly hot with unshed tears of anger and sadness. "I'm sorry...I can't..." I choked out, and snatching up Francis I walked off as quickly as I could.

When I got a little further off I let the tears flow as I walked. Two days ago I had almost fancied myself some sort of creature from a fairy tale. But I wasn't. I was small and naive and ignorant. I'd been sheltered far more than I realised.

What a fool I was to think someone like me could help people such as Janushek and Lily! I couldn't even help a frightened child like Una.

If these were the sorts of things—bigotry and violence and the abuse of trust—that made up the rottenness at the heart of Ormdale, what hope was there for me to accomplish the task I had set myself of cleaning it?

Not much hope at all, surely. Then I recalled the almost mystical feeling that had touched me the previous evening in Drake's library. Surely that must be where my quest lay—to reunite the dragon families. Perhaps then it wouldn't all depend on me. Perhaps even now, a sage imbued with the spirit of Taliesin or Merlin graced the hidden court of this Wild Wales, ready to offer me wisdom.

I was entering the kitchen yard when I stopped short. A scaly iridescence was curled up in the sun outside the scullery door, completely blocking it.

"You greedy thing!" I scolded. Clearly, the wyvern had returned because it wanted to be fed.

I was not in a mood to be trifled with. I stomped up to it and tried to shoo it away from the door. When it didn't move I seized a rug-beater that was close by and swatted it lightly.

It turned and hissed at me. Francis leapt off me and hid himself behind a pail in the corner of the yard.

"Don't you talk to me like that! I kept you alive for a month, ungrateful beast! Now, *shoo*!"

I became aware that someone was leaning out an upper window and watching me. I glanced up and saw Una's large eyes showing over the window sill. She must be standing on tip-toe. I remembered suddenly my promise to be a good example to her.

"Look here," I said to the wyvern, lowering the rug beater out of consideration for the impressionable Una. "You can't stay in the kitchen yard.'"

I fished a very dry piece of gingerbread out of my pocket and offered it to the creature, walking backwards slowly to the entrance of the yard. "You've got to go look for your mate. Go on. You can't just sit about. Show some enterprise."

This time it rose up slowly and began to stalk after me, its ears flat against its head and its eyes fixed on me intensely. I had never seen it take a stance like this before but I was too intent on getting it out of the yard to pay much attention to that.

I saw that Gwendolyn had joined Una at the window and was watching me, though why she found this so entertaining I couldn't imagine.

When I got to the entrance to the yard I planned to step aside and throw the bit of gingerbread as far as I could.

I was just preparing to do that when I happened to glance up at the window and saw to my surprise that Gwendolyn looked stricken. She even had one hand over her mouth. What on earth was worrying her?

At that moment, a strange guttural sound rattled out of the throat of the wyvern. I looked at it. I suddenly knew without a doubt that it was readying itself to strike me. It had drawn back its neck as far as it could and its jaws were opened, displaying all of its teeth.

While confident that I was immune to dragon poisons, I was by no means immune to pain, or to injuries caused by ripping jaws or tearing claws. I wondered fleetingly how much damage it might do me.

I also felt rather hurt that my wyvern was treating me like Julius Caesar on his worst day.

Suddenly, from behind me came a familiar bird-like sound. I swung round.

I froze in horror at what I saw behind me. There, outside the yard and about twenty yards away, was *my* wyvern.

Which—and this should be quite obvious by now—meant that the wyvern which was at present readying itself to attack me was *not* the creature I had tenderly cared for by hand all those weeks.

Rather, it was a wyvern whose acquaintance I had made a few moments earlier by the intemperate application of a rug beater.

I felt a rush of air behind me: the attack! Staggering aside, I put my arms up to protect my head and face, but nothing happened. I looked tentatively round.

It appeared that the angry wyvern had flown up to perch on the wall of the yard to peer with interest at its counterpart.

My wyvern returned its gaze and gave another lovelorn call. Then it extended both wings and trotted back and forth twice in an obvious display of its charms. It was now clear to me that this was the male.

The female eyed him from her perch above me. The male bobbed his head up and down; a little desperately, I thought. I was beginning to worry that she was not the marrying kind, and I hoped that in her boredom she would not suddenly recall my recent offences and descend in wrath upon me.

Just to be safe, I crept backwards a little in the direction of the scullery door.

All of a sudden, the female made a decision. She hopped down from the wall, on the outside this time, and ran past my wyvern rather provokingly—finally disappearing in the direction of the river. The male wyvern hesitated.

"For heaven's sake, go after her!" I hissed. With this encouragement, the wyvern hot-footed it in pursuit.

Just then Gwendolyn appeared at my side.

"Shall I get the brandy?" she asked.

"I think I need something stronger."

"Tea, then," she said grimly, "*and* cake, I think."

"Such recklessness in one so young! But yes. Most definitely."

Chapter Thirteen

"I shocked you last night," Gwendolyn said perceptively as we drank tea together.

"A little," I admitted. I found that after an almost sleepless night and the events of the morning so far, I no longer had the resources to be angry at Gwendolyn. And what kind of friend was I if I could not allow for the vast differences in our upbringing? "I told you once before, it doesn't shock me when babies are had out of wedlock; that's all in the Bible, after all. It's...the particulars, in this case. I've told Lily that I'll be paying Pip wages, and I'm going to see about him getting at least a bit of an education."

Gwendolyn sat up very straight and poured more tea.

"It's what we should have done years ago," she said briskly.

"You were afraid of your father, weren't you?" I asked. It suddenly all made so much more sense: Una's fear, Gwendolyn's fear, Violet's cheerful conviction that violence and death lurked around every corner.

"Yes. I was. I never thought about it that way. But now you say it, I think I was always at least a little afraid." She said this almost wonderingly. "When it's there all the time, one doesn't realise it—quite. Like a bird who's never known anything but a cage, I suppose."

At that moment I lost all impatience I had felt towards Una for her timidity.

"I expect it might take a little time, Gwen," I said softly. "To stop being afraid, after all those years."

Our eyes met and I felt her face relax a little, as if I'd given her my approval to allow the wounds time to mend.

"In the meantime, I'm not sure what else to do about Pip," I said. "But Father will know, I'm sure. I imagine the boy himself should be told at some point. How strange to grow up like that, a different person than what one thought."

Gwendolyn snorted faintly and cut me another piece of cake.

"Who knows if any of us are what we think. I daresay there have been more than a few babies in bedpans and such in the history of any really old family like ours. Look at the royal family, after all."

I looked at her in astonishment. Was this all the upper classes really were? People who knew deep down inside that they weren't who they pretended to be?

"That's what's so comforting about anatomy," she said in a tone of deep satisfaction, sitting back in her chair.

I was startled. "Anatomy?"

"Yes." Gwendolyn's face became really cheerful now. "It doesn't matter who you think you are, you still have a tibia. Your lineage may go back to King Arthur or King Arthur's stable hand, but if the doctor makes an incision, you bleed, whoever you are—and what's more, you bleed red."

"Never blue?" I asked jokingly.

"Never blue," Gwendolyn said firmly. "Now, I know I was beastly about that missive from King Arthur's court, but if you really want to go I won't be beastly about it anymore, I promise."

"I really want to go. I'm sure they must have answers that we've forgotten here. But even if it turns out they don't...I must know for myself. I'd always be wondering."

She considered me for an instant. "Then you should try to take Simon," she said at last.

"Try? I don't imagine it will be very hard. He's as excited about it as I am."

"I know that. But do you really think Helena will let him?"

"Let him?" I was a little surprised. True, I was waiting for my Father's letter before I made firm plans to go, but though my parents had counselled and cautioned me, they had not forbidden me from doing something for many years. "I thought you told me that Simon stood up against everyone, when they wanted to force marriage on the two of you? What makes you think he wouldn't do the same about this?'

Gwendolyn was suddenly occupied collecting crumbs from off the table. "That was all his father and mine. It wasn't Helena's design. In fact, I'm quite sure she never intended me for her son. I should think Simon will find it rather harder to stand against his mother's wishes than he did against his father's."

The idea of Helena forbidding Simon to go with me to Wales was somehow offensive to me. I had recently seen Simon exercise excellent judgement in difficult situations. Surely he could and would make his own decision about this?

Then I remembered the last thing he'd said to me last night. *There are things I love here.*

I almost blushed again. I had taken his words to include me. But he might have been speaking only of his mother. Perhaps it was her that kept him here.

"You don't like her," I said all of a sudden. "Helena."

Gwendolyn shook her head. "It's not that. It's...I think—I think I am afraid of her."

"Afraid?" I was astonished. How could one be afraid of a woman who never left her own bed?

"It might take me some time to stop being afraid," she repeated my words, almost apologetically.

"Of course. I'm sorry. I think I might go see Simon later."

"Be careful at Drake Hall, won't you," she said, as if the words slipped out quite unintentionally. But the words were familiar. She had said the same thing to me before. At the time I'd thought she'd been referring to the stranger who turned out to be Janushek. Now I wondered if I'd understood her at all. What was I to be careful of at Drake Hall?

We heard the sound of hooves and cart wheels on the gravel outside. That would be Thomas, come back from the village with the mail.

"Oh, let's see if there's a letter from Father," I said eagerly.

There was no letter from Father, but there was one from Dr Worthing that rather excited us.

Dr Worthing wrote to tell us that he would be holding a charitable dispensary in the village on the following day, and that if Miss Worms was not otherwise engaged, she might profit by observing it.

Miss Worms was both ecstatic and terrified at the idea and went off to cram as much anatomical knowledge into her head as she could, though I protested that he couldn't be expecting her to operate on anyone on the following day.

I was saved a trip to Drake Hall by Simon himself riding up on Portia with Pilot trotting behind as we finished our midday meal.

George ran out onto the terrace to stroke the horse's neck. Simon swung down gracefully as I came out to greet him. I bent down to greet Pilot. He was a delightful dog, and would have been even if he hadn't also saved my life.

"I thought I might have a look at that saddle in the Muniments room," Simon said to me.

"I'll go with you," I said. "I'd like to fetch something from there anyway." I was suddenly eager to talk with him again about our discovery and plans.

"Mr Drake, will you teach me to ride?" asked my brother all of a sudden. "All my cousins know how, and I don't."

"I will be very glad to, George." He looked at George thoughtfully. "I think you will be good with horses. Here, take her along to the stables now." He handed my brother the reigns. "Give her a pail of chaff and sit near her as long as you are able. Horses are easier if they have grown accustomed to your smell, you know." George led Portia off, Pilot following him companionably.

The two of us climbed up to the little door which led from the rooftop to the top room of the octagonal tower. We went in.

I breathed in the smells of the dried herbs in bunches, the beeswax, the books, the musty old smell of the scales and feathers of the specimen cabinet. The choke of dust was gone, happily.

Simon looked around him. "This is beautifully done."

"The children and I got very dusty, and had a lot of fun hunting through everything. Who wouldn't want to be let loose in a magical chamber like this?"

He looked at me admiringly. "I wouldn't have thought anyone not born here would have taken to all of this as you have."

How close his words were to Mrs Worthing's that day—but she had been speaking of how hard it would be for Simon to find a wife. I brushed away the thought.

"Here it is," I said, showing him where we had stowed the saddle. "It's not for a horse, is it?"

He knelt down and examined it, stroking the decorative leather tooling with his left hand, the one with the missing thumb joint. I wondered how it felt, and—not for the first time—how it had happened, but I didn't like to ask.

The design was of entwining leaves, and very beautiful, in a style I had seen nowhere else. Or had I? Was there something familiar about it after all?

"The girth is much longer," he pronounced, interrupting my thoughts. "And the saddle itself is...wider. It's not for a horse."

He looked up at me and I felt a thrill of excitement pass between us.

"And I've only ridden a donkey at the fair for a penny," I confessed ruefully.

"I have the greatest confidence in your ability to acquire new skills," he said, smiling.

"Will you teach me?" I asked. "Like George? So that if the time comes, I'll have ridden something other than a donkey?"

"It would be my honour," he said lightly, and this time I didn't feel as if he was saying it to a saint. Perhaps my plan of inoculation was working after all.

"Will it cost me a penny?" I teased as I unhooked a hanging bunch of the herb Artemisia to strew about the kitchen yard to discourage lurking wyverns.

"No. Not a *penny*." And the way he leaned ever so slightly on the last word almost sounded as if he was reserving the right to ask for something else in payment.

I glanced at him sharply. Goodness, was he *flirting*? I wasn't sure I entirely liked the idea of Simon flirting, even with me. He was so steady and sincere about everything; I didn't want him to change.

But he looked perfectly innocent. I must have imagined it.

We left the room and went out onto the narrow walk on the roof. After my conversation with Gwendolyn, I had fully intended to tell him how much I wanted him to come with me to Wales, but suddenly I lost my nerve. I was afraid it might be interpreted as being of more significance than I intended.

"I've had a very trying morning," I declared, in absence of anything else to say.

"Your father is well, I hope?" he asked, concerned.

"Oh, I'm sure he's well. It's just...every time I think I've got to the bottom of the mysteries of this place, there's something else. Some new secret. And they aren't always pleasant ones, like that wonderful room." I gestured behind us, then leaned on the parapet to look out over the valley. Simon said nothing in response.

"Don't tell me you have some terrible secret you've been keeping from me," I said, laughing at the absurdity of the idea. My laughter faded quickly when I saw his face. "Oh, Simon, no!"

He raised his eyes to me reluctantly.

"I'm afraid there is something."

It really was too bad, when I'd thought Simon *at least* was someone I could trust not to have any dark secrets. But what could I do but laugh about it, especially when he looked so ridiculously like a guilty schoolboy?

I threw my hands up. "*Et tu, Brute?*"

"It's not terrible, but it is something I've been very much wanting to tell you. Or show you, rather."

"Right. Where is this thing you're going to show me, then?" I looked about me impatiently.

"Tomorrow night. Come to the Hall an hour before sunset."

"It's something that only comes out at night?" I quavered, remembering the night we had chased a wyvern about in the moonlit ruin.

"Not really even then. You won't be able to see it. But you will hear it." His voice was now very serious.

A chill ran down me.

I remembered Gwendolyn's warning. *Be careful at Drake Hall.* Was this what she had she been trying to warn me about?

Chapter Fourteen

Simon's brow furrowed. He was staring past me.

I followed his line of sight towards the fells. I could see someone riding down from them, fast towards the Abbey.

"He's in a right hurry," said Simon.

It certainly wasn't normal to see farmers galloping down from the fells. We couldn't yet make out who it was, but I knew that the bridle path went past Talbot's Farm, and not much else.

"If—if a child gets bitten, does it damage them faster than an adult?" I asked.

"Yes."

"Talbot has children, doesn't he?"

"Six."

We looked at each other. With one accord we hurried downstairs to wait in front of the Abbey for him.

Simon was calm but I could tell from the tension in his jaw that something was really amiss.

"Edith," he said.

"Yes?"

"If someone has been bitten up at Talbot's, could you be ready to ride behind me? Right away?"

I took a quick breath.

"Yes, of course." I said it, because what else could I say? Yet I had no idea if I could even get up on the creature.

The rider wheeled his exhausted and muddy mountain pony to a stop close by. He took his hat off.

"Please, Mr Drake, it's our youngest..."

"How long since she was bitten?" Simon interrupted.

"We didna' know, we all had the fever, we kenned it was nowt but that..."

Simon steadied the pony and gripped the man's arm in one movement.

"Steady now. Ben, how long?"

The man's face crumpled and his shoulders sagged.

"Yan day. I came as soon as t'wife saw t' marks.'"

Simon's face went still. He stepped back and whistled some kind of signal. Immediately I heard the sound of hooves on the gravel and Portia came cantering round the corner of the Abbey, homing in to Simon like a falcon returning to its handler.

He was in the saddle in a heartbeat, and turning, he stretched out his arm to me.

The combined height of the horse and Simon seemed immense to me, dark against the sky, but I stepped forward and lifted my arms to him in a step of pure faith.

The farmer appeared behind me to give me a helpful if undignified shove. Simon's arm that I was clinging to went tense like iron and suddenly I was very high up indeed. I'd instinctively flung my leg over the horse. I made a hasty effort to arrange my skirts so a minimum of my undergarments were visible.

"You'll have to hold on to me," Simon warned. "I can't hold you while I'm riding. Are you ready?"

I didn't think I was anything like ready, but I nodded my head, and he must have felt my chin jut into his back because he made a soft clicking sound to the horse and she went. She seemed to go from still to gallop in no time at all. My stomach did the same.

He needn't have told me to hold on. I clung to him like a limpet, with nary a maidenly misgiving. I didn't open my eyes. The drumming of hooves pounded in my ears. The world tilted under me this way and that. I had no idea how I was still on the saddle at all.

"Edith." He was shouting but I felt rather than heard his voice. "There's no time to stop and open the gate. We're going to jump when I count to five. Just stay close to me. It might help to shut your eyes if you're worried."

Stay close! If I could have gotten any closer, I assuredly would have. The bit about closing my eyes made me gurgle into his coat, which I suppose he took as a sign of comprehension.

"One....two....three.....four...five."

At that point the pounding stopped and I felt us leave the ground. I felt oddly detached and free. I wished we wouldn't come to ground again. But then unforgiving gravity wrenched us back, my teeth jarred, and the galloping started again.

I don't know how long that ride was. When we began to slow down and I heard Simon talking soothingly to Portia, I opened my eyes to see a farmyard. We stopped. There were people at the door, an older girl holding an apron to her face.

"Edith, we must get down now," Simon's voice said inside his coat, which now seemed a permanent part of my cheek.

I realised I was still stuck to him like a barnacle on a ship. I let go, but I couldn't feel my fingers. Simon got down and reached up for me. I slid down into his arms clumsily.

He held me steady and then took me inside quickly. I saw a clean farm kitchen and a peat fire with an orphaned lamb sleeping in a box near it, and then we turned sharply into another room. There were several children lying in one bed. They looked hot and unwell, with bright pink cheeks.

There was another bed with a very small child in it, in her nightdress, perhaps only four years old. She was shaking. And she was pale, as pale as death. A woman crouched beside her, holding her hand.

The first and only time I had healed someone from dragon bite, it had been a full grown man, and he had been bitten only moments before.

This small child had been bitten a full day before. What if it didn't work? What if I couldn't heal her?

The woman looked up at me, and I knew by her face that she must be the mother.

"Please, will tha help 'er?" she said.

Simon's hand was still on my arm. He tightened his hold on me. It was a warm, encouraging pressure and it helped me to recover myself.

"Where is she bitten?" I asked, and my voice sounded normal.

"On 'er back," the woman said. Simon helped her to gently turn the child over. She lifted the nightdress and I saw the place. Just two scarlet spots on her deathly pale skin, between her shoulder blades. No wonder they had missed it, and thought she was suffering from the same fever as her brothers and sisters.

I leaned over and spat on the marks. Then I got out my handkerchief and carefully rubbed the saliva into the spots, as I'd seen Gwendolyn do that eventful night. I had no idea if more saliva would have superior curative effect, but I did it again anyway. And then again, a third time.

Simon put his hand on my arm, very gently. "It is enough."

I believed him. He had seen his own mother do this many times. He took my arm and drew me back out to the kitchen where he sat me in a rocking chair by the low-burning fire. He knelt down and mended the fire himself while the girl with the apron gave me a drink—I think it was ale. It tasted strange and dark. The lamb in the box stirred in its sleep. I could hear someone crying. I wanted to cry myself but I thought that would be too much, so I didn't.

After a little while, there was a slight commotion and the mother came out of the bedroom carrying her child in her arms. The mother looked so much like a renaissance painting of the

Virgin carrying her dead Son that I thought the child must have died.

"Mercy," she said. It took me a moment to realise that this must be a local corruption of the foreign word *Marsi*. "Mercy, will tha hold 'er?"

Simon must have seen my thoughts on my face. He bent close and spoke quietly so only I could hear.

"They think that you and my mother can heal by touch also. It's a folk belief."

I stretched out my arms.

"Of course," I said. How could I tell her that I was terrified to hold the child, terrified she would die in my arms, instead of her mother's?

She laid the small body in my arms.

I rocked her, and because it seemed fitting when rocking an ailing child by the fire, I sang softly.

Mercy, the mother had called me. *Mercy*, I prayed silently.

The child's shaking stopped. And yet I kept rocking. I could not tell her that her child was dead.

And then—the last thing I expected—the child made a sound; a sleepy murmur.

"Bonny," she said.

I stopped.

"Bonny!" the mother exclaimed. "She said bonny!"

"I think she wants you to keep singing," smiled Simon.

The woman folded the child in her arms, sobbing. One of her strong hands closed round mine and gripped it hard. And I didn't bother to hold my own tears back any longer.

The trip back was far less dramatic—I rode in the cart which had brought the farmer, Talbot, back from the Abbey. Thomas drove me home. Simon rode quietly alongside. I didn't feel like talking, I felt numb. He stayed close but never claimed my attention, supplying a comforting presence.

Now that I was outside and had my eyes open I saw that my skirts, petticoats, and even my legs were spattered with mud. I shuddered to think how much of my person I had displayed to the surrounding countryside on my mad gallop. Fortunately, the surrounding countryside currently consisted of a few cows.

As we pulled up at the front of the Abbey I was dismayed to see another pony cart approaching from the direction of the village, with a gentleman sitting in front next to the driver.

I was hardly in a state to receive a visitor. I was about to spring out and disappear into the house before I was compelled to greet this visitor, when the gentleman in the pony cart took off his hat and waved it about in a familiar way.

Hardly ever in my life had I been so happy to see someone as I was then.

"Father!" I gasped, and jumping down I ran to meet him.

Chapter Fifteen

We hadn't got a letter from him telling us he was coming because he hadn't sent one. He knew how rarely letters came and that he would travel in advance of one just as Mother had. He had set out the day after receiving mine. He had already been considering joining us for a week or so.

A conference with his curate decided the matter.

"He's very ambitious and hard-working, my curate," he explained to Mother and me at tea, after I had made myself clean and respectable again.

The children had gotten permission to eat their tea by the river, Simon had gone home, and Gwendolyn was still frantically anatomising; so it was just the three of us, and very snug we were.

I don't know if it was the ride or healing the child that did it, but I was tucking into Cook's baking with a will. And I was very happy to be sitting in a comfortable chair after the day's adventures, which had left me as wobbly about the legs as a new lamb. And it was comforting to listen to parish gossip for a change.

"You know the wealthy young widow who has recently joined the parish, my dear," asked Father.

"Mrs Rowntree? The intellectual one?" said Mother.

"I believe my curate's sudden solicitude for my health and thus his desire to relieve me from sermonising for a month may be due to her." His eyes twinkled a little.

"What?" I said, laughing. "Does he think she'll fall in love with him because of his *sermons*? He'd far better have kept his mouth closed!"

Mother seemed to agree with me. "Did you tell him, my dear, that his best points are not appreciated from the lectern?"

"I did my best, but he was quite determined. I suppose Mrs Rowntree deserves to know the worst, after all."

"He reminds me of my wyvern," I remarked between bites.

"Does your wyvern have clerical aspirations?" asked Father.

"No, he has conjugal ones, like your curate. Hopefully to be soon rewarded. Speaking of the wyvern only, of course."

"Ah, yes," said Mother. "The ritual display. You told me about it. I think if your curate were to adopt the wyvern's methods Mrs Rowntree would be most grateful for the visual barrier the lectern provides, as indeed would the entire congregation."

"I admit I am confused, but I trust that you do not speak irreverently, my dear, of ecclesiastical furnishings," Father smiled at mother, his eyes twinkling.

Between laughter and cake, I was quite incapacitated.

"Of course not, dear," responded Mother sweetly.

I wiped my eyes with my handkerchief.

"Oh, Father!" I laughed. "It does me good to see the two of you together again." I drew his arm through mine. Mother had his other arm.

"You've been having adventures, I hear," he said.

"Yes. But I want to have another," I said opportunistically.

"Your account of the mysterious invitation was most intriguing. I suppose you've found the location on the map by now?" he conjectured.

"Yes!"

"And worked out how to get there?"

"Of course."

"Oh, Edith, you haven't!" exclaimed Mother.

"Simon and I worked it out together," I said, which caused Mother to raise her eyebrows slightly.

Father scrutinised me. "You look a little different. Wiser."

"I'm afraid I'm still the same everyday Edith. I've only done my hair differently."

"The same everyday Edith, eh? The same Edith who chased a ruffian alone into a cave to save her brother, and brought him out safely? The same Edith who has been running this estate for me for more than a month? The same Edith who caught a thief, and then galloped across the fells to save a child from a horrible death?"

I had enjoyed my respite from heavier subjects. But this list brought them back to my mind forcefully.

"Oh Father, it has been *such* a day," I sighed, completely sober now. "And I've so many things I must speak with you about. I really thought she had died, the child," I said quietly.

Father took my hand in his. "If not for you, I am told she would have."

There was a moment of solemn silence.

"Father, how on earth did you forget about all this? I know you were only a child when you left, but..."

"I didn't," he said, startlingly. "I never forgot. Not really. It was all there; deep down. But very early on, it was forcefully brought home to me that speaking of it...resulted in punishments."

I nodded. Father had spoken minimally of the beatings he had received at school, but they must have been severe to cause a dutiful child like him to run away as he had. "So I stopped speaking of it. And then after a time, it all seemed like a dream. I didn't have words for it anymore. The Church helped, you know."

"Really?" I exclaimed.

"Well, my dear, there are plenty of dragons in the Scriptures." He smiled. "I think I always knew—in a very secret part of myself—that it wasn't just childhood fancy."

What would I have thought, I wondered, if he *had* told me that he'd lived with dragons as a child? But perhaps he had, and I just hadn't ever really listened.

"Well, my dear, I can't fault you for keeping a secret from me—you told me you saw a dragon in the garden when you were a child, after all," said Mother.

"And so I did! Now, Edith, your mother and I will go up to Talbot's farm tomorrow morning and offer a prayer of thanksgiving," said Father.

I was glad he did not ask me to go with them. I wanted nothing more than to spend tomorrow morning doing as little as possible.

"I'm sure they would like that. I doubt the last squire ever did anything half so kindly. I'm afraid that my uncle's treatment of those who trusted him is one of the things I must talk to you about."

"Tomorrow evening, then?"

"Yes, tomorrow evening."

I woke the next morning in an agony of aching muscles, mainly emanating from the areas of my body which had come in contact with the horse. Thank goodness Mother thought to bring up a breakfast tray.

Francis had reappeared not long after the wyvern went away, seemingly unashamed by his display of cowardice. He sat nearby, patiently waiting for tidbits from my tray. He might not be a reliable defender, but he was a pleasant companion. This morning he behaved a little oddly—tickling my face with his tongue and then gazing at me for a time.

"What is it, Francis? You look like an anxious mother hen!" I laughed, petting him to reassure him I was perfectly all right. My fingers were sore from where I had interlaced them round the front of Simon's waistcoat, and there was the faint impression of a button on my inner wrist. I took up a book and sat by the window to avoid thinking more of that.

I saw nothing of Gwendolyn except briefly out the window when she got into the carriage to go to the village to assist Dr Worthing.

Later in the morning, I heard Portia whinny outside. My heart jumped—had Simon come to see me? But now George ran out to meet him, and it was clear that Simon had come for George's first riding lesson.

If he'd offered to give *me* one I would have thrown my book at his head from above. But he only nodded briefly at me when he saw me at the window and went back immediately to teaching George.

He had a curious way of doing this. There was no saddle and no bridle on the horse, only a simple halter and a long rope such as one uses to lead a horse to pasture. Simon held the end of the rope loosely as Portia walked in a circle around him on the grass. He pivoted comfortably on the spot, giving George an occasional direction or encouraging word.

Without the conventional accessories of a rider, George seemed to encounter some difficulty staying on the horse's glossy back. He hunched forward and gripped the mane nervously. But as the morning wore on, George began to sit more upright and adopt a looser posture. I saw that as the animal's powerful muscles moved, George's body moved in concert with them.

I remembered how I'd watched from the riverbank and seen Simon and his horse as partners. George was a long way off, but suddenly I could see why Simon would choose to teach him this way. It was as if by removing the conventional tools of man's mastery over horse, a rarer and more enduring relationship might be attained.

I marvelled again at the way the animal trusted Simon, her ears twitching in response to his voice, and at Simon's gentleness towards her. He had called her a friend. She was nuzzling him now, and he touched his forehead to hers.

Oh, dear, I was watching him again. I shook myself and got ready to leave my room.

I was in the sitting room with Mother and Father when Pip came in with the exciting news that the river dragon's eggs were beginning to hatch. We all threw on some outdoor things and followed Pip to where he had left George and the girls watching this unfolding wonder.

There was a spring in Father's step and a gleam of excitement in his eye, not to be quenched by Mother's reminders to be careful of his rummy ankle.

"I may be older than you, my dear, but I am still only forty-three!" he protested.

All six of us crouched in the rivergrass as the river dragon emerged with a wrinkle and then a rush of water. The tiny dragonets had worked their way out of their shells. She carefully but authoritatively took them into her jaws, which she kept ajar. Then she swam downriver with them, quite unconcerned when she passed us. The hatchlings looked like tiny wriggling omnibus passengers.

After she'd gone there was a burst of general excitement, with George making all sorts of learned observations about the habits of freshwater crocodiles, to which I am afraid I paid little attention.

I was thinking again of the man I had met on this riverbank, and the depth of anger and sadness hidden behind his impudent manner. I thought of Lily and Pip, of the injustice and cruelty of their lot. What future awaited either of them but drudgery and loneliness? I was hit again with a wave of heaviness, like cold water pulling at my skirts, dragging me down.

Suddenly, Una spoke. This was so rare that we all quietened and paid attention to her instantly.

"There's one left," she said, pointing.

We all followed her outstretched arm. Sure enough, back among the litter of recently-vacated eggshell, there was movement. Violet and George, being the fastest and least desirous of maintaining cleanliness, went and fetched it.

Violet held it out to us, pinching it by the nape of its neck with thumb and forefinger, half dangling. It had tiny aquatic fins, struggling legs, and a pitiably thin body.

"It will die, I expect, without its mother," she declared.

Una was staring up at it with a mixture of repugnance and pity. Suddenly I couldn't bear the idea of giving up on it.

"Couldn't we take care of it? Like an orphaned lamb?" I remembered the lamb in a box by the fire up at the Talbots' farm.

George looked at me in sensible surprise.

"But Eddie, we wouldn't know what to feed it."

"Well, George, I hadn't the faintest idea what to feed Francis when he hatched and I assure you I never considered leaving him to starve," I said, a little severely.

I was surprised to see Una looking at me, her eyes shining a little.

"We are dragon keepers, after all," put in Father. "And *the righteous man hath regard for the life of his beast.*"

"We might at least try," agreed Mother. "It will be very good for you, children. You can record its development in your nature books. Pip can sketch it for us. But we'll need one of you to agree to care for it."

"Una, would you do it?" I asked, on an impulse. What a strange idea it was—when I knew perfectly well that Una was afraid of dragons.

Una blinked a few times. Then she turned to Violet and mutely held out her pinafore, just as if she was collecting daisies to make a daisy chain. Violet conveyed the squirming dragonet into Una's possession.

In an instant all of the numb heaviness that had gripped me a moment before evaporated.

What was this feeling? Hope.

What had mother said? *Courage is love defying fear.*

I had just watched a frightened little girl enact those words. Perhaps there was hope for the orphans and the wanderers after all, if a child like Una could stand taller than her own fear and welcome one.

Gwendolyn returned just after tea-time. She collapsed in an armchair in the sitting room while Lily was clearing the things. I wasn't sure what to make of Gwendolyn's expression. She was tired, certainly, but there was also an energy about her that I couldn't quite interpret.

"Lily, would you send Pip round to the Lodge for me? I'd like to see Dugdale as soon as possible," she said. When the two of us were left alone, I moved my chair close to Gwendolyn.

"Well?"

"Oh, Edith." Gwendolyn passed a hand over her face.

"What? Was it awful?"

"No! Yes. I mean, in one way it was awful. In another, I've never felt so completely alive." Her hand left her face and I could see that her eyes were bright. "We set up in the vestry of the village church. People waited in the pews and then I would call them in to see the doctor. You should have seen their faces when they saw me! The squire's daughter. I suppose they knew how Father would have felt about it if he'd been alive. Anyway, there was a little table in the vestry and the doctor wouldn't let me put anything on it. I soon found out why. It was a free dispensary, you understand—it was quite understood that the doctor didn't want any payment. But everyone who came in put something on the table." She shook her head in wonder at the memory. "At first it seemed comical to me. There was a cheese that was put there, a pot of honey; that sort of thing. If the consultation was dull I started to guess what people would put there. Sometimes they put coins. But then I began to see it differently. A man came in whose clothes were full of holes. He had a sick child with him, whose clothes were not much better. That man put down a coin. The doctor gave it back to him and told him to buy some beef to make beef tea for the child. How I wanted to give him the cheese!" She looked at me. "You see, Edith, all this time I thought medicine was solving mysteries, trying to see inside people for what's wrong with them—like trying to catch the criminal in a detective story. But it's not just that, it's not just nerves and glands and things—it's the people themselves." Her eyes were almost burning now. "Dr Worthing talked with me afterwards. He says that most of the ailments that he's seen in Ormdale are simply due to poverty." She stood up and began to pace. "All this time I've been wanting to learn how to cure diseases, and I've been completely ignoring the people who suffer from them."

There was a knock on the door, and Dugdale showed himself in.

Gwendolyn turned to face him, immediately all business.

"Thank you for coming so quickly, Dugdale."

"I weren't far, ma'am," he replied.

"Your plan to start a limeworks on the estate—I'm sorry I haven't paid more attention to it. So you'll forgive me if I ask you to repeat yourself."

Dugdale inclined his head.

"Would the proposed industry, do you think, employ a sufficient number of men from Ormdale to improve the living conditions of the poorest families of the Dale?" she asked.

If Dugdale was surprised by this question, he didn't show it.

"I've no desire to overstate my case, ma'am, but truth be told, I don't doubt it. The living conditions among the common people of Ormdale are such that almost anything would improve them."

Their eyes met and I thought that for the first time they began to understand each other.

"Then blast it," Gwendolyn said, her chin high, as if she was defying someone who wasn't there.

"Ma'am?" There was a touch of incredulity in his tone. I almost hooted—I had now seen Dugdale thoroughly surprised, and by Gwendolyn, of all people.

"Isn't that how you get the stuff out of the ground? Blasting?" she asked innocently.

"Why, yes, ma'am, that's right."

"Well, then, as far as I'm concerned, you may let the blasting begin. The sooner the better."

"I'll go and explain the plan to the new squire now, then, if I may."

"Do that."

Dugdale left, with more of a spring in his step than I'd thought possible for such a rock of a man. Gwendolyn leaned on the mantelpiece. She looked as if she had laid down a heavy burden.

"Edith, more than anything in the world, I want to be a doctor, and I'm going to work my hardest to become one. But in the meantime, I'm going to try being my own kind of squire's daughter, for a change."

"I expect the Dale won't know what's happened to it," I grinned.

At tea-time, Father read to us from an ancient epic poem, translating the Anglo-Saxon himself as he went. I was surprised and happy to see Violet and Una hanging on his every word. I became rather more interested in this exercise myself when I realised the subject of the epic: a creature the Anglo-Saxons called *draca*.

"There was a hidden passage, unknown to men..." Father read. "For three hundred winters he had guarded the underground treasury..."

"Three hundred years!" I protested. "But that's impossible!"

Father looked at me mildly.

"You don't object to a dragon guarding treasure, my dear? Only to the longevity of his occupation?"

I shut my mouth. I wasn't sure what I objected to anymore. Helena's stories of her family's history had given me grounds to believe that there was something to the idea of dragons guarding treasure, after all.

Helena! In the excitement of the last day and a half, I had completely forgotten my promise to meet Simon before sunset.

An hour later, I received a note from him via Pip. It warned me to dress warmly and for a ramble, and not to bring Francis. A ramble? At twilight?

Another revelation was looming. I felt a mixture of anticipation and exasperation.

I'd promised to talk with Father this evening and now I would have to put that off. I wasn't exactly sorry to postpone revealing to Father the perfidious behaviour of his own brother. But it wouldn't be any pleasanter a task tomorrow.

I'd also hoped to get Father's blessing for a trip to Wales. But since healing the Talbot child I was beginning to doubt whether I should leave the Dale at all during dragon season. If the Talbots had been forced to carry her all the way to Helena's bedside for healing, would she not have perished on the way?

Perhaps I needed the extra time to think, after all, before unburdening myself to Father.

I asked Lily to tell Father I was going on an evening walk. Then I put on several layers, along with my macintosh and stout boots, and did something no respectable clergyman's daughter would dare to do: I went out to meet a young man at sunset.

As I did it without a qualm, I realised I wasn't a clergyman's daughter anymore, not really.

No. I was the same Edith Worms, but she was a Marsi and a Worm Warden now, and whatever secrets still lay hidden in this valley were rightfully hers to know.

Chapter Sixteen

Simon met me just before I got to the Hall. I noticed he hadn't brought Pilot with him. Then it was as I had suspected: we were going to meet a dragon tonight.

"Thank you for coming," he said.

We walked upriver towards the Great Rock.

"I believe you know that Queen Elizabeth entrusted Bartholomew Drake with a dragon that was found aboard the commandeered Spanish galleon, the *San Salvator*."

"Yes. Your mother told me that it retreated to the caves, and it was thought that led the Drakes to hide their treasure there."

"That is right, but it is not all," he said. "This dragon was neither a European dragon nor an Oriental one."

"It was from Spain's colonies in the New World, wasn't it?"

"Indeed it was. And it was not just any dragon. Have you heard of the giant winged serpent, the protector of the Aztecs?"

"I think so. Didn't it have a name that was very difficult to pronounce?"

"The Quetzalcoatl."

We were now entering the desolate ravine where lay the entrance to the labyrinthine network of caves I had once braved to find my brother. The leafless ravine was even more forbidding than usual in the fading light.

"Where are we going?" I asked, feeling a little chilled suddenly.

"Above," he answered. I was relieved. I had no wish to enter those caves ever again, and certainly not at nightfall.

Simon showed me a better way to climb out of the ravine than the shingly slope I had scrambled down once before. It was certainly pleasanter to traverse this desolate place with a companion, and one who seemed to sense so unerringly when I wanted to refrain from conversation.

When we reached the top there was colour in the sky, and the giant cobbles of the natural pavement stretching out before us reflected the rose tints above it. I had never been here before at day's end, and I caught my breath at the lonely beauty of it.

Lights were kindling in the distant Abbey windows. I remembered that this was the place which had first stirred a love for the Dale in me.

"We have a little distance to go yet," said Simon.

I turned and followed him towards the fells. It was not yet dark, but the moon was already rising, and it was full.

"Simon, won't you tell me exactly what I'm going to see?"

He faced me. His eyes looked even darker than ever, if it were possible, in the twilight. "I don't think you'd believe me.

I wouldn't have believed it myself, if someone had merely told me."

"All right, lead on," I yielded.

Ahead of us was a curious place I had only glimpsed before from a distance: a depression in the ground, about the size of a churchyard. The landscape around us was virtually treeless because of the strong winds which buffeted it regularly, but in this relatively protected spot some trees had found a toe-hold. The area was guarded by a rock wall. I had been warned that there was some topographical feature that made this place unsafe for grazing animals and for humans, but I wasn't clear what it was and had assumed it was a bog. I'd heard Dugdale and Gwendolyn speaking of bogs and sheep getting stuck in them.

Simon seemed to be heading straight for this place, which with its circle of stones had almost the air of a fairy ring.

"Isn't there a bog in there?"

Simon shook his head. "No, it's a sinkhole—the Dale people call it a shake-hole."

"A sinkhole!" I repeated in dismay. "And we are walking towards it in the gloaming?"

At this moment he was holding out his hand to help me over the wall. "You will be quite safe; just stay close to me."

An unexpected sound met my ears. A cow lowed mournfully from behind a tree inside the circle.

"What is a cow doing here?"

I took his hand and clambered over the wall. The cow, it turned out, was tethered on a long rope. We approached it, and Simon surprised me by patting it a little wistfully.

"Simon, if this is your secret pet cow I really think we might have saved ourselves a lot of trouble and come during the day..."

He turned and looked at me. "I feel sorry for it. Because I'm about to feed it to a dragon."

"Feed it..." I looked around me a little wildly. A single dragon big enough to consume an entire cow was not a creature I cared to meet in a lonely grove at twilight. It was almost dark now, and I thought I had never found myself in a more haunted place. Where on earth had Simon brought me?

"This isn't—this isn't a *sacred grove*, is it?" I whispered, suddenly chilled to the bone as I recalled that lonely groves had been used in ancient times for pagan sacrifice. I knew that the pre-Christian inhabitants of the Dale had such practices. I moved a little closer to him.

To my surprise, Simon laughed. "Oh no, it's nothing like that."

The full moon was now above us, framed by the circle of trees. I froze. Almost one of the very first things I had learned about dragons was that they were especially active during the full moon.

"Simon, where is the dragon?" I managed.

"Below us," he said. I couldn't understand his meaning.

"Come." He held out his hand. I did not need to be persuaded to take it.

We moved carefully closer to the centre. He stopped and pointed, but I had already seen the yawning hole, fringed with ferns, into which the earth seemed to be slowly collapsing.

My skin was suddenly tingling with fear, remembering myths of the Underworld, of Persephone snatched away from daylight, of the Minotaur imprisoned beneath the palace. Of legends even more foreign, where temples deep in equatorial forests dripped with human blood. I shook myself.

"Now what?"

"We wait."

"For what?" I whispered.

He didn't answer.

It was a very still night. Suddenly I heard and felt movement from deep within the earth.

I stepped back hurriedly.

"Don't be afraid, it can't get out. The opening isn't big enough," Simon reassured me.

"Isn't big enough?" I stared at him, not at all reassured. The hole in the ground was enormous. How big must this creature be? "But what about..." I glanced back at the cow.

"I have to lower it down."

"Alive?" I cried, aghast.

"That's how my father did it. But I can't. I shoot it first," he said shortly.

I felt the movement of something subterranean under my feet. Something gigantic. Something hungry. I took another step away from the hole.

"When?"

"Now."

He moved the cow closer to the opening, drew a pistol from his overcoat pocket and quickly dispatched it. I saw now that the cow was not tied to a rope only, but a whole pulley system attached to the branches of the tree closest to the sinkhole.

Simon took off his coat. He dragged and pushed the heavy bovine body until it was dangling over the edge. I stood back very unhelpfully and watched with an attitude of silent horror. He untied the other end of the rope and began to slowly ease the body into the hole. Despite the pulleys it looked a thankless job.

I could just faintly make out the whiteness of the cow's body descending in the moonlight. It must be at least thirty yards below. Then it vanished into darkness.

After a moment's more lowering, Simon tied off the rope, slipped his coat back on, and came to stand beside me. We both peered down, not venturing very close to the edge. I could see nothing but the taut rope, yet I found it impossible not to look.

Suddenly there was a snapping sound and the rope jumped and went slack. It was as if the creature had been devoured whole.

We looked at each other.

"You said there was one dragon found on the galleon," I demanded. "How is its descendant here today if there was only one?"

"Precisely. There was only one, and so it follows that this one cannot be its descendant."

A heartbeat passed.

"Simon, this isn't...are you telling me...but it's been..." My blood chilled as I calculated the distance in time. "Three hundred years," I finished rather quietly, thinking of Father's epic.

"It has to be the same dragon, you said it yourself." His voice was tense, and I heard a plea in it to believe him. "It's the winged serpent, the Quetzalcoatl. It has to be, Edith."

For a moment there was nothing but moonlight and a breath of wind between us. I had seen Simon vulnerable before, but never this vulnerable.

All at once I understood. *How good you all must be at keeping secrets,* I had said to him, carelessly. This was *his* secret, and he was risking revealing it to me. At this moment, it mattered tremendously to him what I said.

"Simon," I said sternly. "I want you to know that if anything happens to you, I am not going to feed your pet for you."

I could see by the flash of white that he broke into a grin.

"You did say that surprise was a welcome characteristic in a friend," he reminded me, his voice ragged with relief and laughter.

"I think you took it a little too far," I objected. I waved my hand towards the pit. "After all, how am I ever to equal this?"

"Edith, I've told you before, my faith in your ability to surprise me is quite unbounded."

Then something strange happened.

I suddenly had a very odd impulse—possibly the most unexpected impulse I had ever had in my life up to that point. I wanted to kiss him. Which no doubt would have really surprised him, possibly surpassing even his performance for me tonight.

I was not entirely sure I could reach his face, even if I stood on tip-toes. Perhaps if I gripped his coat collar. Needless to say, I did not act upon this impulse.

Instead, I pulled the collar of my own coat up and said, "Simon, if the deed is done, oughtn't we to be walking home before my reputation suffers any further?"

I thought he startled slightly, but I couldn't be sure. He seemed rather somber as he led me out of the place. I was wondering how he was expecting to get us back down that ravine without breaking my neck in the dark when he picked up a lantern from beside the wall and kindled it.

Then I saw his face, and it was indeed taut with concern. I hadn't just imagined it.

"What is it?" I asked.

"I must apologise. I am not always aware of what is considered…respectable in the wider world." He looked really embarrassed now. "Gwen and I were permitted to be in each other's company at all hours, you see."

"Ah, but then everyone thought you and Gwen would be married, didn't they?" I only realised what an awkward comment this was once I said it.

"I think you must have a question for me, after what you've seen tonight," he said, and I was relieved that he had not pursued the other subject.

"I have more than one!"

"The question I keep coming back to is the one you taught me to ask: *why*. I've been asking myself the same question. And I think I may have the answer. As you have observed yourself, the children of our respective families are somewhat given to following instructions blindly."

I was feeling cold and light-headed. We walked across the pavement and I saw to my great relief he was going to take me home via the sheep paddocks on the same side of the river as the Abbey, instead of the more dangerous ravine.

"But there must have been a very pressing and particular reason why my ancestors chose to go to such lengths to contain and keep alive a foreign dragon with such a prodigious appetite, don't you agree?"

"You think it was because of Elizabeth?"

"I think it must have been. Think of it. At the height of England's fear of invasion by Spain, a very special dragon fell into our hands. A dragon which the Aztecs believed would have protected their nation, had it not disappeared just before the conquest by the Spanish."

I shivered. I had remembered something too.

"Simon, do you know that Elizabeth had her own court astrologer and ordered auguries performed before a battle? I found it so curious when I read that—for a Christian monarch at the beginning of the modern age to be so superstitious. It's possible she really believed that the dragon offered England some kind of protection... Simon! Remember, she chose a dragon for her coat of arms."

"And her motto—do you remember what it was?" I didn't. "*Semper Eadem. I do not change*," he told me. "What if even that is an allusion to the long life-span of the dragon? To its fidelity in its role as guardian? Perhaps Elizabeth took it as a model for her long reign?"

"But Simon, I have another question. This creature—it must have been the one that killed my uncle and his son?"

"Yes," he said shortly.

I shuddered. I had myself recently been an unwilling explorer of the caves wherein this giant predator resided. Unlike my two unfortunate relatives, I had escaped its wrath.

"And it was my fault," he said. I could hear the ache of self-blame in his voice.

"No! How could it be?"

"While he was alive, my father insisted on keeping the creature a secret, even from your family. But last year, I told your uncle about it."

"But why would he—"

"It was the treasure. He hadn't believed in it before. It was just a story, one of the many folk tales in Ormdale. Once he found the Drake dragon was real, he was convinced the Drake treasure was real, also. And then he couldn't rest until he'd found it."

I stumbled. I was suddenly feeling very, very tired—almost faint. Simon steadied me.

"Simon, is it very cold?"

He held the lantern closer to me and looked at me with concern.

"No, not very."

"I—I think I'm unwell."

He laid his hand on my forehead and it felt like ice.

"You have a fever. Dear God, what a brute I've been to drag you out here!"

"No, it must have been the Talbots. The children. They had a fever, remember? Is it much further to the Abbey? I don't mind walking, but I do feel so very cold. I hope Lily won't mind lighting a fire for me, even though it is June."

Simon took off his overcoat and wrapped me in it. It was more than a foot too long for me.

"I don't think I'll manage a country ramble in this," I laughed feverishly.

He solved that by picking me up. The rest of the journey home was indistinct as I rapidly became more ill. My head was aching terribly.

Someone must have seen Simon dramatically descending from the fells with me in his arms, swinging a ghostly lantern, because when we got close to the Abbey there was a rush of people to help. There were lots of feet crunching on the gravel and concerned voices, among them Mother's. They were telling Simon to hand me to Thomas, and I knew how exhausted he must be from carrying me all that way. Then I was carried inside and upstairs and said, "Thank you, Thomas," feeling proud of myself that I wasn't too feverish to be polite to a servant, but I looked up and realised it was still Simon carrying me.

It was he who laid me in Mother's bed like a child at last.

Apparently I slept for a day, sometimes fitfully, sometimes feverishly. I was not aware of the passage of time but I had strange snatches of dreams. I dreamed of Elizabeth, who looked like me, with hair like angry flames. And Simon saying "I do not change," but it wasn't about Elizabeth, it was about him. And then Elizabeth was ordering me to be thrown into the pit, so I wasn't her anymore, but someone else. And I asked if I could feed the winged serpent with rats instead, and I lowered them down on a fishing line and jerked them about. But I fell in, and was lost in the dark for a while, as I had been when I was searching for George.

I found Helena, sitting on a throne, and her eyes were sad. I realised she was Persephone, stolen from the sunlit world to rule over an underground realm of dragons. There was a man, waiting behind her throne, shadowy and dark, whose features I couldn't make out. She wept and begged me to stay with her because she was lonely. And suddenly I was afraid that she wouldn't let me leave.

It was then, I suppose, that my fever broke.

When I awoke, Gwendolyn was sitting with me.

"Hello, Edith. How do you feel?" she said, laying her fingers on my wrist most professionally and looking at her watch. It felt odd to have her look after me, instead of the other way round.

Francis was watching me from a patch of sunlight on the window ledge.

"Exhausted." I reflected. "Thirsty."

She placed another pillow under me and gave me a drink. I marvelled at how naturally she seemed to do it.

"I hope you appreciate that I did this just for you," I said.

"How considerate," she said, measuring something from a medicine bottle into a spoon.

"Weren't you worried about me at all?" I complained.

"Oh, I didn't need to be. Your sweethearts were worried enough."

"My what?" I squeaked.

She nodded towards the nightstand.

On it stood a profuse bunch of lemon-coloured snapdragons which made me smile instantly. There was a book with it, a volume of Jane Austen. Curiously, there was also a jar of rather cloudy water tied round with a bit of string. Gwendolyn saw my look of utter confusion and took pity on me.

"The flowers and book are from Simon, obviously. The jar of unsanitary river water is from the other one." She turned it helpfully around so I could see that attached to the string was a scrap of paper with RUSALKA scrawled on it. "He absolutely insisted it would make you better," she said acidly.

I burst out laughing. And then I felt exhausted. "I think I'm making another friend. It's surprising how easy it becomes once you make a start." I yawned. I snuggled down into the covers. I felt something cool brush my neck. Francis was curling up against my shoulders.

"I see. Having made friends with me, you've now moved on to befriending thieving vagrants of uncertain ancestry. Very flattering."

"It's not uncertain at all. He's Jewish," I murmured half into the pillow.

"See what I mean!" she retorted. Then stopped with a stricken look. "Oh. I'm sorry, Edith. How stupid of me." She put her hand on mine impulsively.

I didn't rush to assure her it was all right, as I would have done once. Janushek's speech in the paddock had made me look at such jibes quite differently. Instead, I squeezed her hand weakly. Then I fell back asleep.

When next I woke up, I found Father sitting by my bedside, reading.

"Hello, Father," I said. "I'm hungry."

"How fortunate that I've been given a tray for you," he smiled at me. There was a bowl of bread and milk on the tray, which he helped me move into a comfortable position. I felt like I was back in the nursery, but not unpleasantly so.

"Has anyone else been ill?" I asked, taking a mouthful.

"Not a bit," he answered. "Not even Mr Drake."

I blushed at this. Simon was the one I'd been thinking of, as he had carried me for so long.

"Your mother and I think you've been run ragged—tending dragons, running a household, writing your book. And various mishaps and adventures."

He was probably right. I hadn't had a really good rest in months. The fever had caught me in a weakened state.

"Given this state of affairs, the two of us have come to a conclusion."

I stared at him. Father didn't usually speak to me this way.

"We think that you should take a holiday. Somewhere away from the cares of both the Dale and our parish. Your mother suggested the seaside. But I had a better idea." His eyes were sparkling. "I hear the Welsh mountains are most refreshing this time of year."

"Oh, Father!" I beamed at him.

"Now then, don't spill your bread and milk," he chided me gently. Something about being tended and watched over like this brought tears to my eyes. I'd been trying so hard to watch over Gwendolyn, I hadn't stopped to think that I might need caring for as well.

"I feel like a little girl again," I admitted. "I'm so rarely ill."

"Do you remember when it was the two of us, alone in the world?" he asked softly.

"Of course. I don't really remember her—my mother."

He gave me a long look. "Have I not spoken of her enough to you, Edith? Is there something you'd like to know?"

Was she sorry to have left her people to live among those who hated them? But how could I ask such a question? It would surely cause him too much pain.

"I don't know, Father," I said, embarrassed. "It's easy to forget, when Mother is here with us and so marvellous."

"In point of fact, there is something I want to tell you about her—about your real mother."

I was surprised. "Yes?"

"You know my interest in languages."

I smiled to myself at this modest statement. Languages were Father's passion. He would have thrived in an academic career in philology, had circumstances been different.

"I've been reading a book by a chap called Conway. He's written about the Umbrian dialect."

"In...Italy?"

"Yes, Umbrian is one of the many local dialects which will likely suffer under the cause of Italian unification, I fear. That is by the by, but I was most interested in his comments about some of the speakers of Umbrian."

"Oh?" I could tell this would take a while to reach any recognisable point so I recommenced eating my bread and milk.

"He described a people of the Fucine Lake region. Their pagan ancestors worshipped Angitia. Do you remember her?"

"Did I know her?" I asked blandly.

"I suppose not, my dear, you never were a very enthusiastic classicist. She was Medea and Circe's sister, and very valued by these Italians for one particular gift: that of healing snakebites."

I stopped eating.

"The people of this place, the descendants of the worshippers of this goddess, are called Marsi."

"No!" I breathed, setting down my spoon. Thoughts began to spin through my head. I seized onto one. "But Father, what on earth has this to do with my mother?"

"Well, what do you know about your mother?"

"I know that she was of the Jewish race."

"She came from a very old family of English Jewry, as they are called. Hers was one of the first families to return to England from exile when Oliver Cromwell lifted the bans on their living here and pressed for toleration for their customs and mode of life. Ironic, is it not?" I stared at him. "For Cromwell to be urging tolerance?"

"Never mind that, Father, what does all of this have to do with the Marsi?"

"Have I never told you? Your mother's family came from Southern Europe, my dear. To be more precise, from Portugal and Italy."

Chapter Seventeen

After Father left me alone I lay still and considered this startling information.

My shock of flaming hair I had believed to be an inheritance from my mother's side of the family. I knew that in general it was considered by the English middle classes to be a sign of low birth. In doing charitable work, I had even visited slums and seen people who shared my hair colour in conditions of direst poverty.

But since discovering that it was a sign of my gifting as a Marsi, a rare born healer of dragon poisons, I had begun to feel differently about it. Seeing Helena's hair united with her undoubtedly aristocratic bearing had also had an effect upon me. Gwendolyn had told me that the colour appeared now and then in the family lineage, and was prized.

I had grown to see my hair as a sign of my honoured place in the new life that had been waiting for me here in the wilds of Yorkshire.

To summarise, I had embraced the estranged family of my father, and in doing so I had never felt more distant from the estranged family of my mother. That shadowy entity had seemed ever more irrelevant as I became engrossed in the concerns of Ormdale.

And yet now it seemed quite possible that they were not irrelevant at all. Could it be possible that within my veins flowed not just one but *two* bloodlines connected to dragons? It was almost unthinkable. Yet I was thinking it.

I now knew of at least one other dragon family in Wales. Why not more in Europe? This account of the origin of the word Marsi would seem to suggest that they existed—in the past, at least.

I felt more than ever determined to make contact with our Welsh counterparts. Every bit of knowledge I could gather must be useful in reconstructing the secret history of the dragon families—and charting their future.

The next few days I was the model of a well-behaved invalid. I had little more than a week to spare before I must be off to Wales to arrive by the date indicated on the invitation, and I did not mean to imperil the trip by any rashness. I moved back into my room and rested as hard as ever I could. Helena had *The Mabinogion* sent over to me and I read it through again to search for clues, refreshing my palate with Jane Austen every now and then. Father told me everything he knew about the Welsh language, which he called Cymric, and I listened as best I could.

"Do you know the Welsh had their own law code, quite apart from our common law, until quite late? Let me see, I think it was one of the Tudors who put a stop to it, for all that they were happy to claim Welshness when it suited them."

I made a mental note to not mention how cozy our family had been with the Tudors.

"They didn't have primogeniture like the Norman English, you know. Everything got divided up, between all the sons, no matter whether you were born within wedlock or without. An estate such as Wormwood Abbey would never have existed under Welsh law."

This gave me a jolt. I'd completely forgotten my intended conversation with Father about the true identity of our housemaid's son.

At that moment Lily came into my room, her presence adding immediacy to my vague sense of guilt. Ever since our meeting about Pip's wages and schooling, a softness had crept into her expression towards me. I didn't think I deserved it. Wasn't I a Worms? Didn't I continue to profit from her pain, however much I might wish to exclude myself from such a sordid story?

"Miss, Mr Drake is asking if you'd be well enough to see 'im."

I was dressed today, and sitting up in bed, with Francis curled up beside me, and I longed to talk to Simon of our Welsh trip. He was the only one who really shared my enthusiasm for it.

"Oh, yes, of course, please send him in."

Father got up.

"I shall leave, my dear. This room would be rather cramped with two visitors, I think."

I glanced narrowly at him as he slipped out. The room was reasonably spacious, in my opinion.

A moment later Simon entered. He had sent wildflowers up for me almost every day; I rather dreaded him appearing with a bunch clasped in his hands like a schoolboy gone a-wooing. I needn't have feared. He carried something wrapped in a bit of wool, and he looked serious rather than mawkish.

"Aunt Emily says you are much better," he offered, a little woodenly.

I was surprised to hear him refer to Mother in this familiar way. But I supposed they must have become better acquainted during my illness.

"Yes, please sit down. I'm feeling rather well, I just wanted to be especially careful not to over exert myself."

He sat down, but oddly he didn't look me in the eyes. "Please, take as much time as you need."

"Simon, is something wrong? You are very solemn today."

"I apologise. This brings back unhappy memories for me. My mother was very ill with influenza, ten years ago. That was when her long illness began."

Of course. Here was I, ill and in bed, with a pet dragon. I must remind him of his mother. No wonder he looked odd and uncomfortable.

I started talking to relieve the awkwardness. "It was the '89 epidemic? I remember it well myself. It wasn't long after my father remarried. He was most anxious about it as he had lost my mother to an influenza some years before. He sent us to the country to avoid it."

"I understand the dread he felt." With those words he finally looked at me. I thought I saw relief flood his eyes and a tension leave his broad shoulders as he realised I was indeed recovering well.

I felt a warmth flow through me at his care. He held out the package to me.

"I've been up to the Talbot Farm to check on the child. They gave me this for you."

Beneath the wool I found a carved wooden lamb of uncommon beauty. I handled its pleasing curves with joy.

"Oh! How lovely. The child is well?"

"Perfectly. She talks of you as of a creature from a fairy tale."

"If she'd seen how I sat on your horse she would be quickly disillusioned." I laughed. "But Simon, I want to know your opinion. Ought I not to leave? If I'd been gone when she was bitten..."

His face grew grave again. He leaned forward with his elbows on his knees and passed his hand over his hair. If my brother had done that I would have smoothed it back. Of course I couldn't do that to Simon. Then he brought up something unexpected.

"Do you know how long my mother has had Mr Darcy, Edith?"

I shook my head.

"It was my Father's wedding gift to her, thirty years ago. Before that, he belonged to your great-uncle. Mother used to go and visit him at the Abbey menagerie when she was a child."

"The dragon is older than your mother, then?"

"Undoubtedly. I believe he is about one hundred years old. He dates from the glory days, when the Worms had plenty of money and few cares. But I'm getting away from my story."

"Go on."

"Mother says the glasshouse where the exotic dragons lived was her favourite place on the estate. She says there were dragons that would flutter about in the sunlight like butterflies."

I smiled at this charming image. Surely this was what Helena had remembered so fondly the day we talked of the glasshouse. Simon paused now, as if really uncomfortable.

"What is it?"

"Mother told me that she spent her first day of wedded life weeping inconsolably."

My smile vanished. "But why?"

"Because when my father presented the dragon to his bride, she saw he had first removed half of its wings."

"He used to be a flying dragon?" I exclaimed, horrified at the thought of this maiming. I had noted the abbreviated wings and had assumed they were some kind of flightless appendages, like a penguin's.

"Yes. Of course, my father did not mean to be cruel," Simon said. I wondered if he really believed it. "He considered it a practical measure to ensure the creature would never leave my mother, but I've always felt it was a tragic metaphor. Do you know that when she was young, they never let her sit on a horse, or go anywhere without someone to guard her? She had hoped that marrying my father would bring her a measure of freedom." He seemed in an agony of discomfort. I wondered why he thought it so important for me to hear this that he braved the pain at disclosing it. "I suppose she must have realised that things...wouldn't be how she'd imagined, even from that very first day."

Suddenly, Helena's conversation with me appeared in a very different light.

The men have had their way in Ormdale for generations. Now it's our turn, Edith.

I felt suddenly horribly sorry for her. Having been tyrannised her whole life, no wonder she saw no other way to live than by wielding power over others. Might I have responded differently had I understood this before?

"Why are you telling me this story, Simon?" I asked.

"Because I don't want it to be yours." His dark eyes met mine unblinkingly. His jaw was set.

"How could it be?" I asked.

"Edith, it is hard for me to say this. I want you to make your home here—in the Dale. But I couldn't bear for you to be trapped here unwillingly, like my mother was. I'd far rather know you were anywhere else at all, if only you were free and happy."

Again, warmth flooded me. Did this man really care for me so deeply? How wrong I had been to dismiss his feelings as a mere schoolboy infatuation.

"Is that why you wouldn't let Gwen tell me I was a Marsi at first?" I asked softly. "You didn't want me to feel that I had no choice but to stay?"

He dipped his head.

"To me, it seems a heavy burden to bear. I sometimes wonder if healing people hasn't drained my mother of what little health was left to her after her infection. I couldn't bear to watch that happen to—to someone else."

His final words fell oddly, as if he'd been about to say different ones. *Someone else I love*, perhaps?

I chose my own words carefully in reply. "Simon, I think your mother stayed because she had nowhere else to go. But that is not true of me. If I stay, it will be out of love, not fear. You said yourself, there are things here worth protecting."

I raised my eyes to his, and for once, I didn't try to dispel the tension between us. My heart beat strangely. I felt like I was standing on the edge of the river that ran through the Dale, the water surging past my feet. Ought I to cross it? Ought I to cross to his side? If I didn't yet love him, might I allow myself to try?

Might I step at least onto the first stepping stone, and see what happened then?

"I promise I will devote myself to protecting them while you are gone," he said fervently.

"Gone?" I repeated, blinking in confusion.

"Your Father says you will go to Wales."

"Yes, but..." I felt embarrassed. I felt as if I'd taken a step and slipped. "I understood that you were coming with me."

"Oh." He paused. "I am sorry, Edith, but I cannot go with you. My mother has asked me to stay with her."

I didn't believe my ears. "But all the plans we made...surely she can spare you for a few days, Simon?"

"She does not ask sacrifices of me very often, Edith. Please, understand this."

His voice was firm. I felt as if I was hit with icy water. Inwardly, I drew back.

I looked away. I did not want him to see the depth of my disappointment. My eyes fell on the jar of murky river water which was still on my night stand. Never before had I perceived so clearly the appeal of Helena's doctrine: *You cannot trust people to make the right decisions.*

"Perhaps I'll take Janushek," I said impulsively, and not very kindly.

Simon looked a little bewildered. "Your father, surely, would be a more suitable travelling companion?"

I felt ashamed of myself. No. Out of principle, I had rejected Helena's way of managing others. I must not change now. I would not try to use jealousy to see if I could alter his decision.

"Yes, of course, you are right. Please thank the Talbots from me, when you see them again, for the kind gift."

He could tell I was dismissing him. He stood humbly. "Do you have any message for my mother?"

Did I? Helena had once offered Simon to me on a platter, so to speak, as she had also offered to share her power with me. I had turned down both offers. Was it to be war between us now?

"Tell her...thank her for the book."

He bowed his head and left. I suddenly felt like crying.

I was bitterly disappointed, perhaps unreasonably so, to discover that Gwendolyn and Helena had been right about Simon. It was certainly not the right time for me to cross the river between us.

Perhaps that time would never come.

Gwendolyn was helping me choose my things for the trip when Martha came in with a package from Drake Hall, large and soft inside its wrapping. I opened it to find the green gown, the Guinevere gown as I thought of it, which I had worn there to dine after I fell in the river. Wrapped up inside was a wide comb. There was also a note.

Edith,

May you find what you seek in Wales.
Helena

Gwendolyn fingered the gown. "It's lovely, but not very practical."

I folded it tenderly and put it in my case. "Which is exactly why I'm taking it. A person who writes a letter on vellum in the year of Our Lord 1899 is not concerned about practicalities," I said definitely.

"Well, that's true enough," she agreed. We both noticed that Martha was still there, immovable. A woman as substantial as Martha does not hover.

"Excuse me, ma'am."

"Yes?"

"Will the *offcumden* be staying much longer?"

"If you are referring to Janushek, I hear from Dugdale that he finds him very useful indeed, especially in setting up this new business with the limeworks. You of all people should know how understaffed we've been for years, Martha."

Defiance sparked in her eyes. "There's plenty of men in the Dale could be hired, ma'am, instead of a Jew-foreigner like that."

Gwendolyn turned sharply on her. "I must insist that you do not speak of him again in that way. He has a name, and you will use it when referring to him in my presence. If you choose to speak in that coarse way below stairs of course I cannot stop you, but I warn you, if he complains to me of his treatment in this house I will listen to him most seriously."

Martha left the room.

"I'm sorry you had to hear that, Edith."

"I've heard things like that all my life," I said shortly, going back to sorting my things.

Gwendolyn blushed, no doubt remembering that she had said something not dissimilar herself only a few days ago. "Doesn't it bother you?"

"It never used to. But somehow, it does now."

There was a moment of silence.

"I suppose I should be glad Father is coming with me. He'll be so ecstatic over meeting Welsh speakers, we are sure to make a good impression. A little national flattery never goes amiss."

I was putting a brave face on it, but I felt rather flat about the trip now that Simon wasn't going. It was like rehearsing a duet with someone and then having to play your part alone for the recital.

Gwendolyn looked at me keenly. "Don't be too hard on Simon," she said.

"Why should I be? You warned me this would happen. I ought to have listened."

"Does he know how much he's disappointed you?"

"I don't want him to go to Wales for *me*, Gwen!" I snapped. "I want him to go for himself! Do you know he has a secret ambition to train dragons? And has had for simply years and years? You've seen how he's trained Portia, as well as Pilot. He has a gift, Gwendolyn. He can't just keep...*existing* here, he needs real work to do if he's to stay in the Dale. He's not a child, he's a man. I just want him to realise it, that's all," I ended, rather weakly. I'd said more than I intended, but it was too late now.

Gwendolyn sat down slowly on the bed. "I was officially engaged to Simon for years, but I think you've learned more about him in two months than I ever did. Why don't you tell him?"

"Tell him what?"

"How you feel."

"It would help if I knew how I feel," I admitted, a little miserably. "What would I say? *Come to Wales with me and I might fall in love with you?* That seems a little unfair. What if I don't, in the end?"

"Well, at any rate, I'm quite sure he knows how he feels about you. If you would only tell him how much you want him to go, I think it would give him the strength to defy her."

"I don't want to fight over him with his own mother!"

"Why ever not?"

What had Simon said to me once? *I cannot imagine accepting a love that is constrained or forced.* I also would accept no less. No, if Simon really cared for me, then he would cut the leading strings himself. I would not do it for him.

"I told you. I want him to choose for himself to go with me. I don't want to...transfer him from one owner to another, like a pet!" I snapped.

Gwendolyn's eyebrows arched. "And you don't know if you'll fall in love with him?" she asked, a little drily.

I threw a petticoat at her head.

At that moment we both heard a whinny outside below the window. We paled and looked at each other. Gwendolyn ran to look out.

"Oh, hello, *Simon*, whatever are you doing?" she said in an airy voice, leaning out the window.

I think my heart stopped for an instant. Gwendolyn turned and shook her head at me to let me know he'd been too far from the window to hear us.

I sat down and breathed.

"Oh, you promised Edith a horse-riding lesson. How *nice* of you. Yes, of course she's feeling well enough."

I sputtered indignantly. Gwendolyn waved at me over her shoulder to be quiet.

"Yes, she's just coming now." Gwendolyn shut the window and turned to look at me. Her mouth was set in a line. "Now, Edith. I quite understand you can't tell him everything you told me. But you *are* his friend, aren't you? You know that much?"

I nodded.

"Then for heaven's sake, try to tell him as you would a friend."

This, at least, I could see was a reasonable piece of advice, though it didn't make me like it any better. I went downstairs.

Chapter Eighteen

George was with Simon, feeding Portia an apple, when I arrived. I felt as shy as a foal at the prospect of any kind of emotional scene and was relieved to see George. Simon turned to me and was all business right away. I was almost startled by his matter-of-factness.

"Now, Edith, you haven't time to learn how to ride a horse in two days. But I've been thinking about it, and what is the hardest part about riding a horse?"

I was dumbfounded. "I don't know."

George spoke up. "It's trust."

"Yes. The horse has to trust you. It's the same with any animal — you won't get anywhere without trust. Did you know a horse's trust is particularly hard to earn?"

I shook my head.

"It's because they are a prey animal. They are designed to look for threats constantly, and respond swiftly with flight. It actually makes them singularly hard to ride. We get in the way of their instincts, you see, and when they respond quickly to a perceived threat, we have a tendency to fall off and hurt ourselves, which of course the animal never intends."

He was explaining this all so well that I found myself following him perfectly.

"You think dragons will be easier to ride!" I cut in breathlessly.

He smiled at me, the kind of smile you give someone with whom you share a pleasant secret. We both realised at the same time that George was staring at us with wide eyes.

"George, go and fetch the pony from the stables, you can practise while I'm helping your sister."

George ran off obediently, with a curious look over his shoulder at us.

"Of course, it's still all theory as it applies to dragons, but think of dogs. They are a predator animal and, as long as you win their trust, much easier to train than horses, partly because—"

"Because they aren't always looking for a threat," I finished for him.

"Exactly right."

"So, if I meet a dragon big enough and tame enough to ride, I just have to win it's trust?"

"I don't think you'll find that hard."

"What do you mean?"

"Have you forgotten what you are?" he said softly. "Dragons are naturally inclined to see you as a friend, because you are a Marsi."

I hadn't thought of it in exactly that way before, but he was right. The strange wyvern in the kitchen yard would have certainly attacked anyone else who went at it with a rug beater. In fact, not one of the dragons I had ever met had tried to harm me in any way. I felt an ember of excitement growing steadily brighter inside me.

"I think the main thing we can accomplish today, is to get you up on this animal by yourself," he concluded.

The ember extinguished abruptly.

"Oh. Must I?"

"I'm sorry you didn't have the best introduction. A madcap gallop across the paddocks to save someone's life isn't what I'd choose," he said regretfully. "But I think you must. It's an adjustment — the balance, and the height. Far better to do it here for the first time than in unfamiliar surroundings."

I eyed the enormous horse reluctantly. Simon touched my arm encouragingly.

"Edith, you've mastered far more formidable things than this." He stepped back and smiled. "Why don't you try to surprise me?"

"All right," I said, straightening my back. "I'll try."

"There's only one problem." He was a little hesitant. "It's about a lady's saddle..."

"I don't want one," I said quite firmly. "I want to learn to ride astride, like George. I can't imagine people who ride dragons — if anyone does — would worry about that. And frankly I find it terrifying enough to be on the back of a large animal with a leg on each side of it. I don't at all like the idea of twisting myself almost in half while trying not to break my neck."

Just at this moment, George came back leading the pony.

"George, do you mind if I borrow some of your knickerbockers?"

George stared at me. "My knickers, Eddie? Whatever for?"

Simon threw back his head and laughed at this.

"Oh Edith, I wonder what they'll make of you in Wales."

"Come with me and see," I said lightly.

He was serious immediately. He looked at the grass.

"She needs me, Edith."

So do I.

I almost said it. I wanted to say it. But was it true? And was it fair to him to say it, even if it was? I wasn't ready to cross the river; it would be cruel to make him think I was.

I swung around and went in the house to get changed into my brother's knickerbockers before I could say something I might have cause to regret.

I spent the rest of the afternoon on the horse's back, as I'd seen George do from my window. I wore my shirtwaist tucked into my brother's garment. I looked a bit like one of those lady cyclists in the newspapers, except I had to use George's suspenders to keep it on. Simon behaved as if this were a perfectly respectable get-up for a nice young lady and I was grateful for that. There are some things one does not like to be teased about. I soon forgot most of my self-consciousness in my efforts to stay on the horse.

It wasn't as bad as I'd dreaded. The sun warmed the horse's glossy coat and made it pleasant to touch. Once I got used to it, the animal's gait became a pleasing rhythm under me, its muscles and limbs a marvel of harmonious design. Even its smell was a pleasant one, I had to admit — a little like grass at the end of summer, and much nicer than the smell of dog, which was the only thing I could think to compare it to.

And Simon was an excellent teacher. And now to see up close the way he worked with his horse and George's pony... It hurt me inside a little. It oughtn't to be me going to Wales at all, it ought to be him.

"Simon, I've just had an idea," I said slowly.

"Yes?"

"What if you go to Wales, and I stay with your mother. Then she wouldn't be alone. She likes me, you know that."

"Edith, I couldn't—"

"No, really. Simon. If they are breeding and training dragons, you would be the best person to make the connection. You know so much more about the history of the Dale than I do. About all of this. Please. At least think about what I've said. Say you'll speak with your mother about it?" I pleaded.

He looked away, then nodded. At that moment we heard Gwendolyn's voice from an upper window.

"Edith! What on earth are you wearing?"

Simon and I burst out laughing.

"Just trying out an outfit for Wales, Gwen!" I called up to her merrily.

"I hope you intend to travel under an assumed name, then," she shot back.

"Yes. I was thinking of yours!" I retorted.

I stood once more at Drake Hall. I had timed my visit to coincide with Simon's usual morning ride. I hoped to avoid him if possible. I asked Forrester if his mistress was well enough to see me and he bowed silently and went up to ask.

I looked at the book of Chopin duets open on the piano while I waited. It gave me an odd pang.

Forrester reappeared and told me that his mistress would see me.

"I wondered if you'd come to say goodbye," Helena said pleasantly as soon as I entered the room.

I was taken aback. She must know that I had wanted Simon to come with me, against her wishes. Yet she smiled at me as if no shadow had ever passed between us. I felt unmoored and foolish, like a child who'd imagined enemies in the corners of her bedroom feels when someone brings a light.

"Yes," I said, trying to collect myself and stick to my purpose. "Thank you for the dress, I will wear it with pleasure. But I didn't come just to say goodbye."

"Oh?"

"I came to ask you why you don't want Simon to come with me," I said in a rush. "It will only be a few days, and I think it would be so good for him…"

"You want me to let him go?" she asked quietly, yet with crystalline clarity.

I spoke more carefully now. I did not want to bargain with her for him. "I don't want you to tell him what to do one way or the other. But I don't think it's right for you to stop him going with me."

"My dear, I think you have misunderstood," she said this with such ingenuousness that I began to doubt myself.

"Have I?"

"You've seen my sitting room, haven't you?"

"Yes, a few weeks ago, but—"

"And what did you make of it?"

I tried to recall. "Everything was laid out for you, a fire burning…"

"That is what was *in* the room, but what *was* it? What did it mean? What did it make you think of?"

I forced myself to concentrate. "A shrine," I said, surprising myself.

"Precisely. Do you know, I've not been in that room for eight years? And do you know who takes care of it, and lays the fires? Did you think it a servant?"

"It's Simon," I realised, with a sinking feeling. There was a pause.

"I've never asked him to do it, you know. I hardly ask him to do anything."

She asks so little of me, he had said. But it wasn't true. Maybe the number of her requests were few, but the cost—oh, the cost was high.

"You think your need is greater than mine?" she asked.

"Of course I don't," I answered a little impatiently. "It's his need I'm thinking of."

"Ah, only *his* need. How very good of you to have my son's best interests at heart." The trace of mockery in her tone was not lost on me.

"He's not a child, ma'am. If you don't cut the leading strings—"

"You will?" Her eyes were hard now, hard as slate.

"No," I said carefully. "Not I. He will."

"And why would he do that? For you, I suppose?"

I looked at the maimed dragon on her lap. Simon had taken it as a metaphor for his mother and her crushed hopes. But it could just as well be him. I wanted to cry. These families! Why did they go on doing this?

I lifted my chin and looked steadily at her.

"I won't ask him to. But sooner or later, there will be a choice between pleasing you and following his conscience."

She was listening now, all trace of mockery vanished.

"And then I think, ma'am, that it may not go your way."

For the first time, I saw fear in her eyes. I drew closer to her, impulsively. "Don't wait for that. Do it now, yourself. Give him his freedom, he'll never think any less of you for it. You may find he thinks more."

For an instant, I thought that she was listening, but no longer.

"How dramatic you are, Edith. You sound as if you've been reading too many penny-dreadfuls—or fairy tales. Am I to be the wicked fairy that enmeshes the prince in my spell?"

"You might be the good fairy that frees him. That is for you to decide."

"I have already decided—Simon will not go to Wales."

I let out a breath. There was no reason to stay longer. "Goodbye, then." I moved towards the door.

"Edith," she stopped me. Her voice sounded suddenly quite different—why? Did I hear a note of apology? Regret? "I told you once, Edith, that I would never fault you for pressing your advantage. I hope you'll do the same for me."

I could find no answer to this byzantine request, so I merely inclined my head and left. I walked out through the silent, muffled house. I felt suddenly as if I couldn't breathe in its heavy atmosphere.

Once out the door, I took a great breath of the fresh air, full of birdsong and whispering leaves and the trill of the river.

I looked back at Drake Hall. I had liked the place from the moment I first saw it, but now I saw it not as a snug cabin in a ship or a magical cavern under the sea, but as a place bespelled. And that spell was quietly, slowly, ever so gently draining someone of life.

It wasn't a safe harbour; it was a ship becalmed. And everyone knew what happened to people on a ship like that, if the wind never came.

Be careful at Drake Hall. I had not been careful, and I had paid for my carelessness. Today, I had told Helena that a break with Simon was inevitable, but was I right? And if that day did come, would it come too late for him and me?

Chapter Nineteen

I was tidying up the papers in my study the next day when Pip brought me a note from Simon.

Dear Edith,

No change to your plans. I shall be with you in spirit, if that means anything to you. Godspeed.

Semper Eadem,

Simon

I blinked back tears of frustration with him. *Semper eadem*—as if that was an unmitigated virtue! I suspected he meant it as a message of constancy to me, but it could just as well represent his refusal to change when change was precisely what was needed. On an impulse, I wrapped up the book manuscript which had been languishing on my desk and hastily scrawled a note.

Dear Simon,

What a bore. This might help you while away the dull hours until I come back and tell you about Wild Wales. I hope it will do as payment for the lesson, since you don't want a penny. I wrote it, in case it's not obvious. I'm not a saint or a creature from a fairy tale. I'm a detective novelist.

See, now it's my turn to surprise you.

Your Very Distant Cousin

Edith

I gave the package to Pip and went up to make sure my suitcase was ready to go in the carriage the next morning.

By the time I came back from Wales, Simon would have had time to reflect on the object of his affections being a writer of penny-dreadfuls. Perhaps he'd like to find out what his mother thought of that.

I had told myself only a few days ago that I might allow myself to take one little step across the river.

I absolutely refused to go any further until I knew if he could, in fact, change.

The day of our departure dawned wet, but not too wet for travel. Father and I were to take the carriage to Embsay and spend the night at the Inn there so that we could set off for Wales as early on the 18th of June as possible. It was an unpleasant day. The wind hurled rain at the windows spitefully.

I was surprised when Violet and Una cornered me with something concealed in their combined pinafores.

"We want you to take this with you," said Violet. "But we want you to promise to take it before we tell what it is."

"How mysterious!" I exclaimed. I considered this injunction. "Could you tell me why I must take it, at least?"

Violet and Una looked at each other.

"North Wales is a lawless place," said Violet. "You might not know it, but it is. It was one of our governesses—she told us they were all heathens, anarchists, and musicians out there."

"You want to give me something to protect myself with?" They nodded solemnly. I was moved. "Well, a young woman can never be too careful, I suppose. All right, as long as I can fit it in my bag."

They beamed and brought out an object I recognised. It was the case containing the blow-pipe and darts that Gwendolyn had used to subdue the wyvern.

"Well, that is a somewhat unusual item of self-defence, but I trust it will make Una more calm in her mind," I said, and took the case. "Thank you, girls."

This was not to be the last farewell present I received. I was getting the chatelaine out of my desk to give to Gwendolyn when Janushek appeared, leaning against the doorway of my study.

"I finished the book you gave me."

He tossed a volume from his pocket onto the armchair.

"Oh, I asked Mother to lend you a book, since I am a hardened novel reader. Did you like it? I told her you don't like fiction."

"It was most informative. An English mode of social investigation. You should read it yourself; such a book is possible in no other country but yours."

I picked it up, glancing at the title idly *Three Men in a Boat*. "Thanks, I shall. I will take it on the train with me."

I wondered why he didn't leave, but lingered to obstruct my doorway.

"What if they don't let you come back from Wales, Rusalka?" he said.

"Don't let me come back!" I repeated in astonishment. "This is *England*, Janushek. You can't simply keep people against their will here."

"I'll remember that next time a young English woman orders me to be locked in the dungeons of her family home," he said expressionlessly.

"Oh, well, yes," I faltered. "I see what you mean. But why would anyone want to lock *me* in a dungeon?"

"Many reasons." He seemed to assess them as he looked at me. "And one of them is that you are a magical person."

"I'm not!" I protested.

"Are you not? Can you not heal those that dragons have bitten, using only your own body? What is that, if not magic? I warn you, Rusalka, don't tell them what you are." His voice was surprisingly quiet now. "Or you will not come back to us."

A chill ran down me at this warning.

"I expect they know more about it than I do, and have their own Marsi, as well, more experienced ones than me." I smiled to cover how unreasonably nervous I suddenly felt.

Getting Father and myself and our modest luggage in the carriage was a chaotic affair with so many people saying goodbye to us in the wind and rain, and with me trying to put a collar and lead on Francis in the midst of it. Simon and I had agreed that Francis would stay at Drake Hall while I was gone. It was safer for everyone if my domesticated dragon resided in a household that also had a Marsi in it.

I suspected the note I had received from him meant that Simon would not make one of the goodbye party, and I was right. Still, I couldn't help looking for him, and feeling disappointed that he wasn't there. Had Helena asked him not to come? Was that one of her few requests?

Just as Father was getting into the carriage and I was handing Francis to Pip to take to Drake Hall, no doubt frightened by the crowd of people gathering to bid us farewell and the unfamiliar four-footed animals drawing the carriage, Francis startled and thrashed his tail about. I hurried to calm him. The carriage gave a startling lurch as the horse shied. In the chaos Father lost his footing on the carriage step and stumbled before quickly regaining his footing.

I settled Francis and followed Father into the carriage, pausing only to press the dragon notebook into George's trustworthy hands.

Mother poked her head in the opposite side of the carriage, holding her umbrella. She had a concerned expression on her face.

"George, are you hurt? I thought I saw you fall. Was it your bad ankle?"

I had forgotten that Father had one ankle that would turn now and then and give him trouble for a few days.

"It's nothing, Emily," Father said.

Mother's face said she didn't believe him.

"If it still pains me when we get to Embsay I'll have time for Gwendolyn's Dr Worthing to look at it," he conceded, and kissed her cheek.

My heart sank. Was everything against this trip? Why on earth was I taking my father and his weak ankle into the wild mountainous terrain of North Wales, where my Polish soothsayer said I would be imprisoned?

Father was unusually quiet on the carriage ride, and I began to think it must be because of pain. I had intended to begin the story of Lily and Pip, but I found I had no stomach for it on this miserable day. Ah well, I would have the entire journey to Wales and back to disabuse Father of any remaining illusions he might have about the character of his older brother.

We arrived in Embsay and drove into the inn yard. I watched Father closely as he stepped out of the carriage, which he did very gingerly. We were served supper by the fire as it was unusually chilly. Father said his ankle was not bad enough to see the doctor, and changed the subject.

"Goodness, how does Mother do it," I thought to myself. I was quite sure his ankle was worse than he let on. What had Mother said? That he wouldn't lift a finger to help himself, only others? What did one do with such people? Simon was even worse!

In the morning I asked Father whether his ankle was better and he assured me it was. Thomas had stayed the night also and was ready when we emerged from the inn to take our things the short journey to the station. I had thought we would walk ourselves, but Father got in the carriage, which made me doubt his word about the ankle. I was now dreading the journey I had once looked forward to so joyfully, and felt I was miserably selfish for not having given up on it before. Thomas had deposited our luggage with a porter and we were approaching the ticket desk when I pulled on Father's arm.

"Father, this is absurd. It's no good—you traipsing about the Welsh mountains with a rummy ankle," I said.

"Edith, I'm sure in a day or two—"

"What would Mother say if she were here?" I insisted.

He sighed. "You're right, Edith. I'm so sorry. I wanted this for you."

"I know you did," I said, squeezing his arm. "And I love you for it. But we should go home now before Thomas leaves with the carriage. I don't want to have to cadge a ride on a hay-cart. This hat is relatively new."

I hastened into the street after Thomas. He was getting back up in the driver's seat, but I managed to attract his attention with a wave.

I felt horribly disappointed but I knew I was doing the right thing. This trip was meant to help our family, not hurt it.

Suddenly I heard a familiar voice calling out to me.

"Edith!"

I spun round. I saw a tall man swathed in a greatcoat, sitting on a graceful bay horse. I froze. I only knew one man who sat on a horse like that.

Simon swung down and approached me quickly.

"Am I too late?"

"For what?"

"Cousin Emily said your father hurt himself, and she was concerned you would go on alone."

"Oh, she sent you to bring me home." I swallowed my disappointment. Goodness, did he only do things when people told him to? "Well, clearly you are not too late as you see I am still here."

"No. She didn't send me." He must have left very early. He looked a little flushed and disarranged from haste; his neckcloth was a little awry and I thought perhaps he hadn't shaved this morning. "I came—because I thought you needed me."

What should I say to that? I lifted my chin to look straight at him. I didn't have much time, but I tried to speak honestly and carefully. "Simon, I'm not running off alone to Wales. You don't have to chase me across England out of cousinly duty. But if you want to come with me as a friend, as we planned together, I still want to go. And there's just enough time to get on the train."

I would not—could not—say more than that. He turned and swiftly unfastened something like a bedroll from the saddle, stowing it under his arm. His face was set.

"Then let's go."

I stared at him for a moment, hardly believing him. Was this really it—the break with his mother; so soon and so sudden?

Thomas had got down from the carriage and helpfully taken hold of Portia's bridle as if he knew instinctively what was going on.

Simon was waiting for me to move. There was no time to ask any more questions. Gracious, why on earth was I hesitating like this? I grabbed Simon's arm and ran for the station.

Father, God bless him, had seen it all from a distance and removed only his luggage from the porter's trolley and got a ticket for mine. As we ran past him towards the ticket counter, I hastily kissed his cheek goodbye, my spirits rising fast.

He whispered in my ear and thrust the luggage ticket into my hand. "Godspeed, my dear, and do try to bring Simon back in one piece."

I laughed and continued our dash to the ticket counter, where I got two first class tickets much faster than I have ever done before or since.

I realised just about now that Simon was looking tense because he had never caught a train before in his life. As I led him quickly across the platform I merrily threw over my shoulder to him the same words he had said to me that night by the sinkhole, "Don't worry. You'll be quite safe if you stay close to me!"

I am certain we attracted comments on the platform, mad pair that we were that day.

I got us into an empty railway carriage as the final whistle sounded, and then I fell on the seat across from him. My heart was pounding with the excitement of the dash and the coming journey—the journey to find Wild Wales, with my dear friend.

"You know, for a fellow who signs his letters *Semper Eadem* you do change your mind rather a lot," I said, catching my breath.

Simon looked around the carriage with interest. Then he pulled something out of his bundle.

"You know, my Very Distant Cousin, when I said I didn't want a penny to teach you to ride, I was only going to ask you to play Chopin with me."

He was holding my manuscript! I sobered instantly. Why had he brought it with him? He paused. I was in agony. He shook his head in amazement.

"You're really a published author? Really?"

I nodded.

"Edith. I told you I have the greatest faith in your ability to surprise me. But this is truly marvellous!"

He was actually beaming at me. On the contrary, I thought, it was he who had surprised me.

"Is it?" I asked, a lovely warmth spreading through me. I thought to myself, *The only thing that could spoil this moment is if he asks me to read it aloud to him, or puts it away to read someday later.*

"Would you—would you mind terribly if I rudely ignore you and just read it? Right now?" he asked uncertainly.

"No," I said, smiling like a giddy baby, "No, I wouldn't mind terribly."

I had questions—what had made him change his mind so suddenly? what had made him come with me?—but they could wait.

For now, it was enough that he *could* change, and that we were off on a great adventure, together.

Next in *The Secrets of Ormdale*

Follow Edith and Simon on their quest in
Castle of the Winds
coming in April 2024.
Keep reading for an exclusive excerpt!

Want to keep up with all the gossip from Ormdale?
Go to www.christinabaehr.com to subscribe to
Christina's newsletter.

A Note on the Dragons (and Marsi)

Once again, I have drawn from Edward Topsell's rich and strange *Book of Serpents* for my information on dragons. If anything seems especially fanciful, it is likely directly out of Topsell (example: dragons inhaling flocks of birds from the sky). He is also a wealth of information on herbs and dragons. Traditionally, the herb wormwood (*artemisia*) was thought to deter them. Indeed, he lists such a surprising number of dragon-deterrent herbs, that it makes me wonder why anyone was ever bothered by dragons at all.

But this novel goes beyond the realm of English dragons, and so did my research. The Quetzalcoatl was really believed to have mysteriously left its role as protector of the Aztec people just before their conquest by Spain. I have imagined that it was kidnapped by the conquistadors, only to make an appearance in the following century on a fictionalised Spanish treasure ship which was commandeered by the Drake family. Sir Francis Drake came from a large family, but his nephew Bartholomew came from my imagination. The piratical tendencies are entirely true to history. Characteristically, Sir Francis even stole his family crest (featuring a wyvern) from another nobleman.

Helena's Chinese lapdragon is a nod to the colonial connections of the Dale families. An ancestor of Mr Darcy was probably collected by Sir Anthony Worms, as this was a time of material prosperity for them (piracy again—this time on the unprecedented scale practised by the East India Company). Chinese dragons were believed to fly, though only a small minority were portrayed with wings, which is why Confucius said (in reference to Lao-tzu), "I know that birds fly. I know that fishes swim. But as to the dragon, I cannot know how he can bestride the wind and clouds when he rises heavenward."

The collection of Welsh legends known as *The Mabinogion* was first translated into English by the folklorist Lady Charlotte Guest. The beautiful poem ascribed to the bard Taliesin from which I derived my epigraph is not typically included in the collection anymore, though it was present in Lady Charlotte's edition, which is available for free online at Project Gutenberg.

When I first encountered the mysterious word *Marsi* in the pages of Topsell, I assumed that would be both the beginning and end of the story of elusive dragon-immune healers with magical saliva. Hardly! I soon discovered that the word referred to a real people and language group in Italy, with references going back to ancient texts. As Edith's father explains, this people was associated with a pagan goddess whose help was traditionally sought for snake-bite, and whose cultists were believed to have special knowledge in herbal treatments for such.

I have, I confess, invented the connection between the Marsi people and a specific hair colour. The earliest English Jews were of Sephardic origin from southern Europe, and could have easily mixed with the real Marsi. I needed a visible marker for Marsi in my story, and I had long been interested in 19th century attitudes to red hair. There is a complex but indisputable connection in the Victorian mind between red hair and Jewishness, which sparked my imagination. Dickens' infamous Fagin was redheaded, Trollope's Mr Slope likewise, and Shakespeare's Shylock was performed with a red wig for centuries until theatre productions became more naturalistic sometime in the 19th century. Today, it has been proven that red hair is found reasonably commonly among Ashkenazi Jews (like Janushek), at around a rate of 5% (the worldwide rate is 1-2%), and the massive influx of migrants from that group (along with poor Irish immigrants, 10% redhead) into late 19th century London likely influenced public perceptions.

Sadly, there was a perception that red hair was more likely to be found among incarcerated, poor, or mentally disabled people; so much so that the Pre-Raphaelite painters were abused by critics (most notably Charles Dickens!) for using red-haired models to portray noble characters from the Bible, mythology, and literature. As a redheaded person myself (with three redheaded children), I've always appreciated the Pre-Raphaelites' largely successful attempt to quite literally paint this genetic trait in a more positive light.

About the Author

Christina Baehr has a ridiculous number of children and lives on a hilltop in Tasmania also inhabited by poisonous snakes, which fortunately hibernate for much of the year.

Christina drank her first cup of coffee at age 41 which must have been what she had been missing her whole life because that was the same year she wrote her first novel, WORMWOOD ABBEY, and began her five book series *The Secrets of Ormdale*.

Christina is also a harpist, singer, and composer, and drinks a lot of tea. She loves nice reviews of her books almost as much as Edith does, and you can leave her one if you would like to make her day.

www.christinabaehr.com

Acknowledgments

I'd like to thank the people who particularly helped me with specific subjects I touched on in this book:

Elisa Riddington, my very own clergyman's daughter and childhood best friend; Karen Scharff, who shares Janushek's background and has been so helpful in advising me on writing about Judaism and Jewish experiences; Sue Perks, my "Yorkshire Sensitivity Reader"; and Sarah Downes, who reassured me I wasn't talking nonsense about horse training. If I ever find myself a dragon, I will take it to Sarah and Sam to be trained.

Sadly, I did not need to go far to find people to give me feedback on living with a chronic illness; there are several in my immediate family, including my mother and daughter. I would like to make it clear that neither of them formed the basis for the character of Helena Drake! I'm sorry you have to walk this road, but I'm so proud of all you accomplish.

As always, thanks to two of my favourite writers living or dead—thankfully, you are numbered among the living—Suzannah and Wendee, for playing good cop/bad cop on every first draft (albeit unintentionally).

Deep thanks to my beta readers Claire Trella Hill and Michelle Bollan for their excitement, encouragement, and the probing questions that spurred me to add small but special details that made this novel richer.

Thanks to Shiloh for the magical illustration of Edith's summer of dragons. I love sharing my dragons with you.

And thank you, Meg, for loving this book the best of them all—even though you don't know why.

Finally, thank you to all of the readers who have welcomed my characters into their hearts and lives. I'm so happy to share them with you.

An Excerpt from CASTLE OF THE WINDS

Twelve noon, June 19th, 1899

As I found myself perched on an exposed mountain-side, and permitting a band of roughly-dressed Welshmen to tie a blindfold around my head, I realised that I had thrown myself into the most dangerous situation of my twenty-one years of life.

But I anticipate.

I will begin my narrative exactly twenty-four hours earlier, aboard a train which had departed a remote Yorkshire station that morning.

"Edith, you really wrote this?" repeated my travelling companion Simon Drake for about the fifth time, looking up at me from the manuscript in his hands.

"I really did! Only if you keep asking me I'll begin to wonder which you think too stupid: me, to have written the book, or the book, to have been written by me."

"Neither. It's very clever, and I already knew you were clever. I suppose I shouldn't be surprised at all."

"Oh no, please don't stop being surprised by me, Simon. We agreed it was a pleasing attribute in a friend, didn't we? But aren't you hungry? You've been reading for simply hours."

"Hungry? Yes, I suppose I am." He made no move to get up.

"We have to change trains later, we might dine at the station when we do that. Or we might get something now, in the dining car..."

His eyes lit up like a boy's. "Might we?"

For a moment, I'd forgotten that this was his first railway journey. I smiled. "Yes, we might."

I led him to the dining car. He walked with great concentration. It was quite a sight to behold this tall, capable man studiously avoiding bumping into other passengers as if it was a great art. After all, I'd seen him gallop effortlessly over the Yorkshire fells on a horse he'd trained himself.

The dining car was a marvel to him. I gently guided him away from ordering soup, which I thought might represent a danger to his travelling clothes. While we waited for our dinner I asked the question that had been on my mind since boarding the train this morning.

"What changed your mind, Simon?"

He looked up from his wrapt examination of the salt and pepper vessels. "I thought...it sounds presumptuous now, but I thought perhaps I could be of service. To you."

I felt a splash of disappointment. I wanted him to make this journey for himself, not me. That would show me that he could aspire to a life bigger than the one he had lived so far—a life not wholly revolving around the demands of his mother. But perhaps it was unreasonable for me to expect him to begin by going against her for his own sake. *One step at a time*, I thought, with an inward sigh.

"Was she very angry? With me?" I asked.

"With both of us," he said quietly, and I saw that was all he was willing to say about that. There was something he did not want to tell me—something that had pushed him too far.

"I'm sorry to be the cause..."

"You have done nothing wrong," he said decisively.

"We'll be back in a matter of days," I said a little too cheerfully. "Your mother will hardly know you've been gone."

It was an empty reassurance, and we both knew it. I changed the subject and was prattling on about our plans when the train entered a tunnel.

"Edith," came his voice, very calm indeed, "what is this?"

"I don't know, what does it feel like? Have you found the mustard pot?"

"The darkness."

"Oh! It's a tunnel. We'll be through it shortly," I said brightly, making a note that when Simon was alarmed he sounded particularly calm. What a lot I still didn't know about him, this tall, dark, Very Distant Cousin of mine. Well, if anything was likely to make me know him better, it would be absconding with him to the mountains.

The dining car was bright with daylight again.

"Remarkable," he murmured.

The rest of our journey was both uneventful and delightful. Simon's occasional comments and bursts of laughter as he read my manuscript made it clear that his enjoyment was genuine. I had always been blessed with the literary encouragement of those dear to me, but not always by their literary *sympathies*. My dear parents were great readers, but their tastes did not naturally incline to detective novels which might be fairly described as 'shilling shockers.'

I was surprised by how much his unaffected appreciation of my work touched me. I had told Gwen that I might fall in love with him if he went with me to Wales, but it would be too absurd to allow this to happen on the very first day!

Steady, Edith. The coast isn't clear yet. There's a mother waiting for him at home.

The other item of interest on our journey was the boarding at a station in Derbyshire of fellow passengers who would later become intimately known to us. I first glimpsed them on the platform as I looked idly out the window. One was the kind of woman that is easily noticed by anyone; the other, the kind that no one ever does.

The first was about my age, and dressed to perfection in the latest style—a powder-blue travelling dress tailored to draw admiring eyes to her sylph-like waist, neck, and wrists, with her hat tipped at an exquisite angle. I wondered how on earth she would keep it all clean. I felt sure my own hair was already dusted with coal-smuts. Her hair was quite golden, and she held her head very upright, as if defying any smuts to dare approach her.

Her companion was a small, thin woman of middle-age with a sad veiled hat, the kind of woman whose every motion tells you she has been designated a chaperone. I felt sorry for her instantly. Even an archangel would tremble to chaperone such a beauty, and I did not think her charge was the sort of person to make the job easy.

The chaperone carried a rather large wicker birdcage. The cage was fashioned so that you could not see what was in it. As they stepped onto the train I heard a squawk that sounded like a parrot. Perhaps a suitably ill-tempered parrot might succeed where the chaperone failed, I thought with a smile.

The town of Bethesda in North Wales was a slate mining town with a depressed atmosphere. We were easily able to hire a conveyance to take us from the recently-built station to our accommodation some miles away in the Valley of Ogwen; the driver said he was accustomed to taking climbers there.

Simon and I shared a doubtful glance. From our experience of Ormdale, we expected the Castle of the Winds to be a place equally obscure. Had we come all this way merely to view scenic vistas with a clutch of tourists?

We arrived at Ogwen Cottage as the light was failing. It was surprisingly severe—a farmhouse at the side of the high road, of stark black slate and whitewash. Between the lowering crag at its back, and the lake and high road at its front, it had the feeling of a crossroads, not a place in itself.

As we approached, lights kindled in several of the windows, like the first stars in a night sky. Perversely, the very strangeness of the place lifted my spirits. If this place was a crossroads, it might yet serve to direct us to the hidden land of Wild Wales.

"*Castell y Gwynt?*" repeated Mrs Jones. She, whose Cottage it was, proved to be a warm and capable woman, rather at odds with her environment. She ought to be harsh and silent, like Grace Poole, with a dragon to hide instead of a madwoman. "It's only a few miles from here, up in the Glydderau. And I expect it will be a fine day for a climb tomorrow." She smiled and left us.

I glanced at Simon over the supper table. Mrs Jones's casual way of talking about it unnerved me. I had expected the Castle of the Winds to be almost inaccessible—a quest to be won only at a cost.

"What if we've come all this way for nothing?" I said at last, just as Simon was getting up to go to his room.

Simon considered this. "I wouldn't say *nothing*. At least, not for me." He smiled his slow smile, the one that had surprised me with its sweetness the first time I saw it. "After all, you let me read your novel."

I tried to damp down my smile of delight. Good heavens, what an egotist I must be if *this* was the way to my heart!

"Goodnight, Edith," Simon's warm touch on my hand as he left brought with it a flurry of other thoughts.

I thought suddenly of Helena Drake, alone in her bedchamber, brooding. How foolish I would feel if we returned home with our tails between our legs, having seen nothing more remarkable than rocks.

Well! In this wish, at least, I was not to be disappointed.

CASTLE OF THE WINDS releases in April 2024.

Printed in Dunstable, United Kingdom